CURSED BLADE

T.M. WILSON

Printed in the United States of America

ISBN 978-1-959483-64-9 (sc)

Library of Congress Control Number: 2023909279

History
2024.11.12

CONTENTS

PROLOGUE

There are days that made you just regret getting out of bed. Those days that you wished you would have ignored the sun and just went back to the peaceful land of dreams. Those type of days that you wished you hadn't talked to anybody and stayed in the safe shell that was your home where it was safe.

The sad thing about this situation is that it arrived as the result of my actions and my choices.

At the beginning I thought that even if there could be consequences for my actions that night they might not appear so soon. They would appear eventually because that was how my life worked but I figured that was a problem for that future version of me. He could deal with all the problems I would create.

The job I had been dealing with was too important to care about the possible consequences.

However, now that I am the version of me who must deal with the consequences of my actions, I can honestly say that the past version of me was a jerk. If I somehow got lucky and managed to survive this night, I would definitely have to stop procrastinating and think more long term.

Considering my current position of fighting for my life behind a quadruple-damned night club with my possible killer standing above me watching my terror-stricken face with clear delight and my friend Marcus being of no help given that he had a thick spear of wood impaling him through the heart and coming out the other side of his chest the chances were not that high.

I can honestly say the past version of me did not foresee any of these events happening when he left the office.

I hate this case. It was supposed to be easy. Something I could solve in a single afternoon. Turns out that was too optimistic. I should have been more cautious when I dug up that first body. That should have been a sign to finish the job there.

Instead, I decided to avenge his death and arrest the dark wizard behind it.

Remembering how this all happened is like a punch in the stomach. With hindsight I can see how all these events had happened step by step, but I still couldn't understand how in just in the length of a school week a case could go from simple as could be to extremely complicated with a body count that just continued to rise.

Like the story of Solomon Grundy, it all began on a Monday.

CHAPTER 1

I was in my office in Frankford. It was a simple building. With four walls and two windows that brought light into the room and let me see the streets and the people on them. My office's sign was on the painted white door. It had taken a long time for me to find a title that I liked for it.

Besides the train that rode above on the bridge and the noise that accompanied it the building was an okay place to work.

In the city of Philadelphia there were lots of businesses run by either small families or big businesses that had corporations all over the country. For all the businesses that succeeded there were just as many that were closing down, changing hands, and becoming something else.

To live in this society and have a life that wasn't miserable required a job. There were lots of options with my skillset and so I chose the job that I believed that I would hate the least.

That led me to choose a job as a private investigator.

I started my own business so there was no boss to report to and I got to pick my own work hours so that was one benefit. There was a lot of work for me in the city, so I didn't have to worry about rent. It was pretty easy with my skills and there was also my other job that I had on the side, so even in a slow month I was not in a need for money. However, the downside is that I cannot tell the government about it.

That was also part of the reason why I needed a regular job. On the off chance that someone decided to investigate me they would not question where I was getting my money from.

Hearing the phone ringing I walked to my desk with a blank look. There was always a chance that it was someone who saw my business card and wanted to hire me though there was also the chance that it was someone who found one of my cards and wanted to make a prank call. It wouldn't be the first time that it has happened to me.

My name is Alex Blackwell, and I just wasn't a simple private Investigator. I am a psychic private investigator. In Philadelphia if you were a non-magical and had a problem that was natural or supernatural my office was the one you called.

"Hello? Blackwell Investigations." I answered the phone with a voice full of confidence.

If there were any trait people disliked in a detective or even a regular person, it was a lack of confidence. I had to make them believe that I could solve their problems.

"I want to hire you." The voice on the other side of the telephone said.

It was never good to assume the gender of the person you are talking to on the other side of the phone. I have met clients under one assumption or another before and then they get angry and storm off. Now I ask for their name before jumping to conclusions.

Live and learn is a very apt description of the detective business.

"Alright so what is your problem?" I asked.

It was always good to get to the point early on otherwise people either get nervous and change their minds or they start to ramble on and on.

I was a fan of neither.

People who call me for work are either the type that either have no options left that can help with their problem or they are the types to truly believe in the idea of psychics. That is a rare thing in the world with all the advancements science has made.

People are more trusting in a method that can be observed and tested than believing in mind reading and fortune telling.

Not that I blame them truthfully. To most people in this world psychics excluding television and in movies rarely turn out to be useful. More likely they are just people telling you what you want to hear and using psychology to give responses that are more likely to affect you.

We are treated as a joke. Seen as con artists out to make money by tricking the gullible and naive and for having incredibly convincing lies. Many people doubted the existence of psychics and when you tell people they either think you should be wrapped up in a straight-jacket and sent to a white padded room or you are lying to them.

To be fair to the people though it wasn't like they were wrong. I really was lying to them. I wasn't psychic, I didn't use psychic energy to understand the stars and see the past and the future. To speak with and banish ghosts. I used something else. That something is much more powerful, and some would say a grand deal more dangerous.

That something is magic.

I am a Wizard. Wizard, Magus, Mage, Magi, and Homo Magika were all terms that could be used to describe my species. Basically, it meant I was someone who used the mystical energy generated by the universe to influence things, people, events, and reality as a whole.

The way I saw it was that I had the skills to do what I claimed I just lied about how I did it. I was simply an honest con man.

In my opinion It was like being a mix between John Constantine and Doctor Strange. My personality may not be perfect for dealing with other people, but I was good at fixing problems. However, I lacked the tragic backstory that brought angst and cynicism upon characters like them. That was a good thing in my opinion. I wasn't a fan of brooding angst or deep introspective thinking.

So, what if I lied about the way I did my work. I got the results that were promised, I just used a method I wasn't honest about. This was magic not science, honesty wasn't required.

I am a fraud, but the thing was I truly could help people, so I thought in terms of karma that it balanced out very well.

It was one of the reasons that I worked for myself. With all the detective offices in the world why would I start a business with how risky it is. For the complete autonomy to do my cases the way I liked without having to explain my methods. There is also the fact that I could charge more for doing less work. Afterall who questions the psychic for their methods when they are always right?

The answer is no one.

"Okay what is the problem?" I asked expecting it to be a simple séance or checking if their house was haunted.

I got a lot of cases like that and few that actually were. Didn't stop me from charging them. Cynical people would probably believe they are getting tricked either way, but my belief was if the psychic isn't charging you that is a clear sign you are getting tricked.

"I lost something, and I need help finding it." The voice responded and I nodded getting out my notepad and pen from my trench coat pocket.

"Okay tell me what it is and it's description." I said clicking my pen and getting ready to write.

Finding lost items was super easy and given how important it is to them that a psychic had to be called I bet I could get paid a lot more if they weren't simply going to replace it in a store.

"It's not that simple." The voice said.

I was used to hearing that phrase. Some people were incredibly shy about what they lost. Sometimes for good reasons, sometimes for stupid reasons but in a rare once in a while it could be both. I charged double for those because of the urgency to find the item.

Supply and demand are a big factor in all businesses.

"Do you want to tell me over the phone, or do you have someplace that you are comfortable meeting at?" I asked patiently.

Some people just did not trust telephones and had a fear that the government was listening in. Paranoid types would be the ones to call psychics. They were not the type to trust the police. I had dealt with these kinds of people before they were mostly harmless. For the ones that weren't harmless, well I had magic, and they didn't, so it was an easy fight.

There was no reason to spook the person yet.

It wasn't the first time someone hired me and gave me a contract to do something and not tell other people. Paranoid people were very quick at jumping to conclusions on their own and they got scared and defensive very easily. It was better to let them drive the conversation and make the decisions. It was easier on me too. All I had to do was show up.

All that mattered to me was that I was going to get paid.

At the time I had no idea how complicated this job would get.

This was the event that led me down my current spiral, If I had the power to see into the future, I would not have answered the phone. Instead, I would have conjured a pillow and went to sleep and not answer any call for the rest of the day.

"Yes." The voice said and gave me an address to their house.

I saw nothing wrong with that. There are lots of people who feel more comfortable in their house than they do outside. I am one of those people, but reality and the economy won't let me stay indoors and earn money, so I had to work. Getting up from my desk and grabbing my coat, I was about to leave but I wanted to make sure I looked professional.

This is one of the few things I disliked about the job.

As a detective psychic or not you had to be impressive if you wanted to be hired. Each new case was like a job interview. I had to impress the client so they would hire me. I didn't do well in those types of situations. On the phone I could fake enthusiasm well enough but when it was face to face that was a little more complicated.

Grabbing my wand out of my trench coat I began to cast my spell. I use a variant of latin for my spells. Spell casting is never done in a casters' native language otherwise if you say a word and aren't paying attention you can cast accidentally. If you cast spells in another language accidentally cursing someone is very unlikely unless you got really enraged and switched to it by accident.

The words are a way to channel energy and give a mental image of the effect that the castor wanted to happen depending on how much energy was put into the spell. In a way the words are like training wheels for the young. The more powerful and or experienced you are the less you needed words to cast spells and achieve the desired effect.

In my case, however, the reason that I used them is because it sounded cool and to me that is a very important thing. Aesthetics are important to me. I base my entire style around it. My wand is made of wood from the Ashoak tree. It is a bit longer than the length of a pen. In my opinion a wand was a wizard's version of a combination of a slingshot and a Swiss army knife. It had long distance damage and the more spells you knew the more tools you had.

"Speculum." I said and conjured a mirror.

The mirror is taller than I am so that my entire reflection could be seen. Being five foot eleven it is rare to find a mirror taller than I was if I didn't create it. I will admit that I spent more time than necessary staring at myself and in my opinion, I am clearly handsome. With my raven black hair, sky blue eyes, and a face that looked younger than I actually was.

Wizard and witches aged slower than regular people so that was to be expected. Though it didn't help with clients who were extremely wary of hiring a young detective it made me feel better about myself and that was all that mattered in my view.

I was wearing a black shirt and jeans, black and blue sneakers, and my trench coat was a deep blue that reached shortly past my knees. I didn't wear a tie with the outfit because they weren't very useful. They were often one of the first things that people thought to grab to choke others with. They were also very uncomfortable to wear. I had no idea why people decided that wearing nooses around your neck made you look more professional, but I wasn't buying into it.

The fact that I didn't know how to tie one also factored into the decision a little bit.

For some reason I couldn't help but feel like the trench coat was in the wrong color for the moment. The colors of the coat were changed often either for drama or my mood and right now I wasn't in the mood for it to be blue. Several years ago, I had the coat enchanted for it to fit my needs. It was a favorite of mine, and I was reluctant to change. It was designed to always match my size and to also repair itself if it was damaged from all sorts of problems like magic, age, rain, fire, and the like.

It could also change colors at a thought. This way I could emphasize situations without talking about my feelings on the matter. With a simple thought the coat changed from blue to a tan brown. With that done it was now time to meet the client. I only wished that the case had been as easy as I thought it would be when I first left my office. Going off I had expected to find the lost item, charge more money than was needed and use magic to cut back on resources and wasted hours that regular detectives would spend on the same case. It was supposed to be easy.

I was right in that aspect of course. The beginning of the case was easy, it only got more difficult after that. It was like a video game. The first level was easy but as you go deeper the difficulty increases.

That is the reason I don't play video games that much. I like things to be simple and easy. From what I have learned this case was anything but that.

CHAPTER 2

There are moments in life that never stop being awkward.

Moments where a single moment can make or break the conversation, moments where the wrong amount of empathy or enthusiasm can make it seem like you are either not serious or too sarcastic.

I didn't like these types of moments and I doubted I ever would.

Being a detective meant I had to meet lots of people, make connections, give favors, and a whole bunch of other stuff that had me interacting in and with society and most of the time I didn't have the patience to do it. I found it boring, and it was rare that other people and I had similar interests.

I was fine when things were easy and predictable, and people were anything but that.

They did dumb things for reasons I could never understand and didn't ever want to. Books were predictable as they came with a summary that let you know if you would like the book in advance or not also with an ending you could skip to if you wanted to see how they would end.

I think that was the reason I liked books more than people.

People had their own motivations and feelings and that made them very hard to predict. Caring for their problems was something I found easy, but I didn't like to do it too often as it was likely to make me sad, so I avoided thinking about them.

I parked across the street from my client's house and took a deep breath. I wasn't by any definition of the word sociable. I held people to a scale of if they brought me amusement or if they were annoying me. Even my long- time friends were on that scale.

It is a constantly shifting scale that varies by the day and the mood I am in.

It is another reason why I work for myself. Trapped in an office with other people having to listen to someone telling me what to do was something I would not have enjoyed. One week of that and people would have been cursed left and right. I had seen people working in offices and by the stress on their faces, I was in a better position.

Giving a sigh I opened the car door and got out. One reason why I drive a car when I can use magic to teleport from one location to another is simple. It is to carry my things. I certainly wasn't going to be paying attention to any of my things when I am working when I have a trunk capable of holding it all. If there were ways to make my life simpler, I wouldn't dismiss them so easily.

The neighborhood wasn't anything out of the ordinary. The houses lined up next to each other, children playing on the sidewalk, small iron gates on the porch, and yards full of grass. After walking up to the house and jumping over the gate I knocked on the door and waited. I really hoped this wasn't a joke like the people who order pizza and give the delivery boy the wrong address on purpose.

The outside of the house wasn't anything special. Its bricks were a darkish red, the door was a deep white that looked like it needed to be repainted. The house belonging to my potential client looked like any house in northeast Philadelphia. There was light shining on the inside, so I knew that someone was in there.

Eventually the door opened, and a woman stepped outside.

I thought it might have been a woman on the phone but with the way technology could change people's voices I couldn't be sure. She was five foot eight, had brown hair that went down to just below her shoulders and brown eyes. She was wearing a black dress that was covered by a red jacket.

"Hello?" She asked as she looked at me.

She looked to be thirty-five, her eyes showed her uncertainty, and she kept the screen door in between us. Even if I ignored her eyes her face showed how nervous she was. Having the job, I do it is important to be able to read facial expressions and behavior, otherwise it is easy to get tricked either by a fake alibi or a sob story meant to garner sympathy. I had seen enough movies and read enough books to know what would happen after that, so I worked hard to avoid making such a mistake.

I strove to make sure things like that didn't happen to me. It didn't work out so well this time.

I still curse the past version of me for being an idiot and knocking on the blasted door.

"Hello, I am the detective you called." I told her and watched as her eyes opened wide and she opened the door and let me in.

She led me to a table that was set up with tea and cookies ahead of time.

I was never one to turn down an invitation for free food, so I sat down and took a bite. That was my first mistake. At the time though I thought they were delicious. I had forgotten what cookies that weren't store bought tasted like. I hadn't had anything different since I was twelve.

There was just something about the way homemade cookies tasted that just beat store bought ones in my opinion.

"What is your name?" I asked as it occurred to me that I still didn't know what it was that I was supposed to be looking for.

"My name is Susan Parker." She said as she stared at me.

I wrote the name down on my notepad trying to seem serious while in truth I was thinking about if she had a sister named May, a brother named Ben, and if they had a nephew by the name of Peter.

It took a lot of work for me to not ask.

"So, what is missing miss?" I asked her, keeping half my attention on my notepad to keep up because many people talked faster than I could write when they were nervous, and this woman had all the signs.

I was worried that if I didn't get her talking about her problem and solve it fast, she would have a breakdown either mentally or emotionally. While curious to see it I didn't want to be the main cause of it.

I wasn't Marcus who held that as a goal on his list of things to do in his very long life.

She had bloodshot eyes, bitten fingernails, and was definitely jumpy. It was either nervousness or she was on five energy drinks and was just beginning to crash. I saw it but I wasn't going to point it out. People were already doubtful of me with how young I looked and that I didn't match with America's stereotype of a private investigator. I wasn't old or depressed with an attitude that was bordering between cynicism and depression.

I was more sarcastic and suspicious yet with a never-ending optimism even when it was constantly betrayed.

Being sarcastic now though would not help the situation and it would look like I wasn't taking this seriously. It was times like this that I regretted not having a backstory full of despair and angst. Not truly but it would probably help with making me look like I am more experienced. I did have bad experiences in life, but they weren't any different than other people living in this world.

I started learning magic at the age of twelve and my life became easier.

"My nephew." She said looking down at the table.

I had to try really hard to not ask if his name was Peter, luckily enough I had cookies to stuff my mouth with.

"When did he go missing?" I asked her and choosing to ignore how in my office she said it was "something" she had lost.

Either she thought I would send her to the police to file a report or just not really try hard to find her nephew but take her money. That was why she made cookies and tea to make me feel a connection to her and work really hard to find him.

If I am honest, a part of me blames Susan for the mess I am in now, but I lay most of the blame on myself because I was the one who didn't back off even when the case began to get difficult. Though I had to give it to her for she was clever. Luring me here first with what seemed like a normal case and then giving me free cookies before telling me the truth.

Hand in hand with how she looked I couldn't just ignore her and go on my way.

I had already eaten the cookies and seen how stressed she was. There was no longer an option of leaving here without trying to help. If I did, I would never stop thinking about what happened and if what I did was the right thing or not.

The thing about me is that I had a problem with letting go. It could just be something I read once that I found uncomfortable, and I would remember it years later and it would still bug me. I had a problem with the whole forgive and forget solution too since it would probably take me decades to ever forget what it was that made me feel depressed or angry and I wasn't about to let this case bother my conscience for years down the road. It was also random so I never was sure what would stay with me and what wouldn't, so I was constantly alert for events like this.

I hate that about myself. Especially now when it might be the reason that I am going to end up dead in an alley. Killed by an immortal sadist. That was a terrible way to die. I had a list of ways I would hate to die, and this was near the top of the list.

"He has been missing for three days." She said.

I understood why she called me now. If he was at a friend's house or a hospital someone would have called her. The police require the person to be missing for two days before they will begin searching for a missing person and since they haven't found him she came to me a professional psychic detective.

"What is his name and what does he look like?" I asked knowing there was no backing out and hoping this search had a happy ending at the end of it.

What I didn't know at the time was there would be no happy ending to this job. The next one was even more rough on me and led to my current problems.

"His name is Ethan and here is his picture." She said handing me a wallet sized picture of her nephew.

He was taller than his aunt, had brown hair that was the color of sand and he had brown eyes just a shade darker than his aunt. This would be a great help even if she did not know it.

"I'll do my best to find him I promise." I told her my face hopefully showing her a determined face.

The fact of the matter was that I did not like feeling bad or losing. The money was important but also the fact that I was now emotionally invested in this was important. I would not fail here. Pride and determination kept pushing me forward even after I found the boy.

I just kept pushing and digging deeper into what happened to him and it is why I am now facing what could be the person that is going to kill me. I was sure I was going to find Ethan. That hadn't even been a concern back then. I grabbed the picture and left the table and headed towards the door.

"Thank you." She said and I could see a smile growing on her face.

Science and reason hadn't been helping her so far, so she turned to faith and supernatural power.

I could not stay and watch her burst into tears. She had paid me the first half of my three-hundred- dollar bill and it was now time to fulfill my side of the deal then get the rest of the money later.

CHAPTER 3

After walking out Susan's door there was only one thing that I was focused on. Finding her missing nephew and bringing him back to his aunt as soon as possible.

The first step to that plan was to head back to my house. The materials that I needed were there. I walked down the steps and headed to my car.

It is a two-thousand-and-five black ford. It had been a gift for my sixteenth birthday from my teacher. It would be seven years ago in a couple of weeks.

If I manage to see that birthday I would go on a grand vacation.

I got in my car and drove off. Other detectives would have stayed to look around the boy's room and try to find some clue. Something that would show where the boy had planned to go. If that didn't work, they would then try to find his friends and people he spent time with. I didn't do any of those things because with magic I wouldn't need to. All of that effort was unnecessary. All I needed to do was use a locator spell on him and I would have his location.

I rarely worked this fast on cases. Normally I just relaxed in my office racking up time and after I figured that enough time passed then I would solve the case.

However, the second that the thought passed through my mind I imagined Susan's face. I would do this as fast as I possibly could.

Hopefully the kid had just taken a trip to the library and was trapped as a sinkhole opened up and swallowed the building. That the situation was so bad that only the top of the building could be seen. Unlikely but this was Philadelphia. Groundcrews were always working on fixing one broken down road or another.

A situation like that is what I hoped for as I didn't like giving people bad news. The information that was the somewhat simple part, but it was the actions afterwards that always left me in a bind.

Driving through the city I took in my surroundings as I passed them. I glanced from the people to the buildings to the tress. I wasn't overly fond of any of it. I wasn't a big fan of nature or the outside world. I was happier inside with a book or television. I was fine with leaving nature to the animals and to the people that enjoyed that type of thing.

Going outside was something I did because I had no choice due to my work. If possible, I would love to stay inside all day.

I locked the car and walked inside my house. The house was two floors if you did not count the basement. The living room, dining room, and kitchen were connected to each other, and the upper floor had my room, a guest room, and the bathroom.

It would have been cheaper renting an apartment but that would mean more people around me and that would have been a nightmare. I did not want to have to worry about people walking under me or having music blasted through my walls.

The best part is that it is thirty minutes away from my office depending on traffic.

I walked through the kitchen and headed to the basement door. I pulled my wand and placed it at the bottom left of the door.

"Absconde eos revelare." I chanted three times as I traced a path with my wand from the bottom of the door to the top and then the other side.

I watched as behind the wooden door a white light was shining.

This was to allow me to access my workshop. A wizard's workshop is where he keeps all his grimoires and research. The place where he brews his potions and practices his spells. They are treated as sanctuaries. I heard that others with magical talent used basements, attics, storage units, and sheds. Mine took it a step further as mine is an extra dimensional space where I could practice freely without worrying about the surrounding area.

It was a place of quiet and peace where I kept my coolest stuff. It could in truth be accessed by any room in the house, but I just like to use my basement door as the entrance because it seemed cooler.

When my teacher taught me the spell, I used it for weeks just to move around. What can I say I was very much a fan of the old Scooby doo cartoons where Shaggy and Scooby hid in one door and appeared out of another when running from monsters.

He had created the spell and while I was unsure if others knew of it, I didn't properly care at the time to ask as I moved from one room to another.

When it was finished, I opened the door and walked down the steps.

My workshop was my favorite place in the house. I had designed it the way I wanted it so of course I would love it, but the point was still valid. It was a room that you could simply lose track of time in if you weren't careful.

I had plenty of experience with that.

My workshop is rather large since time and space weren't limitations that you had to consider when working with magic, you could make it as big and as distant if you wanted. You could make it stretch as long as you wanted. Time and space also could be altered to my desire.

In practice it was similar to the hyperbolic time chamber from Dragon Ball Z.

I had shouted down here to test the distance and the echo would travel rather far before dying off.

I had rooms dedicated to keeping my books. Books that I had read countless times, books I had yet to read, and books that I didn't think I would ever read but kept since they were gifts. I had an entire room filled with books that were just fiction about magic and adventure.

There were also rooms filled with projects of mine, some finished and some just getting started.

It was my dream to one day read all the books that I had and complete all my projects.

Those books played a huge part in why I chose to be a detective. Before learning magic, I had spent most of my life reading books about adventures, mystery, and fantasy and I realized that I wanted to live a life like that. After I graduated school, I figured why not try to live my life as if I was one of the characters in those stories.

Well, I can say that I have finally accomplished my mission.

Finding the crystal and map that I needed I began my search for Ethan. Magic just made life so much easier. Unless you were messing around with dark magic or trying to cast a spell way beyond your level of knowledge or power it rarely failed you.

Magic is a mystic force of energy created at the dawn of the universe and generated by all things contained in it. Wizards and witches broke it down into two main categories that we have labeled as prana and mana.

Prana is the energy that is in the atmosphere and the universe that exists in all dimensions, and it feeds magical beings like gods, demons, trolls, and ghosts. It gives them their power and it is created by the life energy given off by living and nonliving things. Prana helped create the soul. It was a pure source of mystic energy which when combined with a body changed it based on that person's body and experiences becoming a diluted mixture.

That energy became mana which was used by witches and wizards.

Mana or aura depending on a person's definition is the life energy created by a person's soul. Wizards and witches have a magical core that is inside of them that converts that energy into magical power which lets them perform magic. Even if you couldn't use magic, you still had mana and each person's signature was different. Wherever you went you left traces of it behind. Mana returned to its original state again when it was cast as a spell.

It was like being a Jedi if you used the original definition of the force, it was everywhere connecting everyone and everything but not everyone could use it.

Another example could be how people and trees exchange oxygen and carbon dioxide with each other.

Using magic, however, was complicated. It required knowledge and training, insight, and creativity, and just a little bit of luck. Lots of people who can do magic either require a teacher to protect them from going too far or being reckless and trying to do too much too soon. Even so, there are still many who tried just that, and it ended up destroying them.

Sometimes metaphorically and sometimes physically.

Magic wasn't contained to certain families and while it is more likely to have magic if you are descended from a family of witches and wizards you can be born with the ability to use magic even if no one in your family before you could. It also wasn't contained to certain ages. Magical talent could be awakened at any age but more often in young people.

Using magic to locate someone whose location you didn't know was a simple thing. There were many types of locator spells, but my favorite method was scrying because I got the location and there was no mess to clean up afterwards unlike if I used something like salt or blood.

I Just needed a crystal tied to a piece of string and a map of Philadelphia.

I began with searching for the strongest and most recent connection of Ethan's mana. The picture was a great help in that task. There is truth in that old belief that pictures could capture a part of a person's soul and so all I had to do was find a strong connection.

There were no words required to do this. I just spun the crystal all over the map and if he was still in the city, I would find him. There was a chance that the kid might have run away. He looked to be about seventeen and teenagers rarely thought things through.

The crystal eventually landed somewhere on the map.

The location was Northwood park. It would take me less than an hour to get to the park.

This is why I loved magic!

Normal detectives would have spent days searching for him and questioning people about where he might be hiding and why he had been missing. With magic, however, I could skip all that effort and get results.

I grabbed the crystal and ran outside to my car. The crystal would point me in the direction of Ethan no matter where he was or how hard he tried to hide.

As I drove there, I couldn't help wondering why Ethan had been avoiding his home for three days.

There were tons of possible reasons, but they weren't that important to me. I had made a promise to his aunt to find the kid and I was going to keep it.

This was my second mistake and led to my next major problem with me spending part of the night in an interrogation room staring down two irate detectives.

CHAPTER 4

Northwood Park is a rather small area and nobody that lived around here would argue that fact. There were parking lots with more space. It is cornered on all sides by a sidewalk and the cement square around it separated it from the street. The place was also rather plain. The park only had grass and trees alongside a couple benches.

The question I asked myself then was what made this park so interesting to Ethan Parker?

The only protection this place gave someone was anonymity. If you went far enough in any direction it would be hard for someone to recognize you depending on where you were standing. This location also served as a bus stop so it would not be impossible to try and blend in as every so often groups formed as people walked on to buses or walked off of them.

Following that train of thought I moved to wondering whether it was possible that Ethan was waiting for a bus.

Waiting for a bus to go somewhere? Maybe waiting here to meet someone? Whatever the answer could be I was going to get it.

It is probably why I was so angry when I arrived and found Northwood park with not a person to be seen.

Ethan was supposed to be here.

I took a deep breath to calm myself. It was likely that Ethan had been here but during my drive over that he accomplished his goal and moved on.

The only problem with that theory was that the crystal had not shifted an inch. It was still pointing at Northwood Park.

Terrible scenarios came to my mind, but I chose to believe that this was just a mistake on my part. That I just located a place where he had stood recently or that I connected to the mana he had when he wore the outfit in the picture. So, all I would have to do is try again and make sure I got a clearer location.

I pulled out the map I kept in the glove box, got out of the car, and walked to the trunk. It had a good flat surface that I could lean on and use. I laid the map down on top of it and began scrying again holding the wallet sized picture of him I was given by Ms. Parker earlier in my left hand.

The crystal started moving as I focused on the image of Ethan and the biggest source of what his mana felt like.

I didn't want to have to go back to his aunt and tell her I failed. Beyond making her feel sad it would be terrible for business.

When my eyes opened, I sighed as I noticed that the direction of the crystal still hadn't changed.

It was time to move on from the opinion that I had been wrong or made a mistake during my scrying. The crystal's location had not changed.

That could only mean that he was here. He was just not visible to me at the moment. Hopefully that just meant he had spent the past few days out testing an invisibility suit that covered a person from head to toe for a startup company. He was not allowed to call his aunt during the testing period.

Maybe it got so comfortable that he fell asleep with it on? I folded the map and put it back in the car.

My feet felt as if they were chained down with cannonballs but there was no turning back. I turned to park and let crystal guide my way as if it were a divining rod.

Looking back at that moment I wish that there was someone nearby to smack some sense into me because the events that followed next were ones that if they hadn't arrived in a specific order, they more than likely could have been completely avoided.

I followed the crystal to a point where it was no longer pointing across the park but pointing down.

With each second my optimism was dying. Unless there was a secret tunnel below my feet that I had no clue about I had a feeling that I was about to discover what happened to Ethan Shaw. With a pit in my stomach, I conjured a pair of gloves for my hands along with a shovel and began to dig in what some would perhaps call a mad frenzy.

It was very exhausting work. My arms were burning, and sweat was running down my face but there was still work to do so I continued. I had no idea at the time how deep he had been buried.

Thinking back given the amount of dirt piled up Ethan had certainly been buried very deep. He had been passed through the dirt and the rocks. Deep through the cement that the government used to build the roads for the area.

Eventually I remembered the fact that I had magic, so I didn't need to actually do the work myself.

Those last two hours of work had been unnecessary. With an enchanted shovel the work could have been completed in twenty. Not much of a surprise given that the shovel wasn't alive, so it did not get exhausted.

However, I wasn't going to do that. After the realization anger and spite had become my fuel. I had already dug too deep to let anything else get the credit.

Ten minutes later I was finished and stabbed my shovel into the ground. If my arms could think independently than they would have hated me. However, I had a deep sensation of pride at my accomplishment.

That sensation could have lasted hours but was ruined moments later when I looked at the body.

Ethan's corpse looked more or less the same as the picture except the clothes were dirtier, the skin was pale, and his eyes were a dull milky color.

"Explaining this to Ms. Parker was certainly going to be difficult." I said out loud.

For instance, how was I supposed to ask for the rest of the money she owed me? I did find her nephew like I promised but he was dead now. That her hopeful dream of a happy ending was ripped in two and that all she had left was the nightmare of her reality.

Awkward would not even begin to describe the situation. News like that could break people.

I was rather lucky when it happened to me and was given options to deal with the pain.

There was always the option of having the police inform her of what happened to her nephew and then mailing her the invoice afterwards.

The idea was discarded. It would remove the awkward situation, but I did not doubt that cashing the check would make me feel uncomfortable.

The only way I could think of telling her any of that is if I discovered what happened to Ethan and avenged his death. This was obviously murder but there were two things about this burial ground that were bothering me.

The first thing that bothered me is the fact that Ethan's body had somehow been buried underground without the land being disturbed. No technology developed on this world would allow that to happen.

The second thing was the symbols that had been carved on to his skin.

On the kid's forehead he had what looked like a star. He was wearing a short sleeve T-shirt, so it was simple to see that there looked to be symbols on his arms as well, but he was too deep for me to see clearly.

I needed to take a better look, so I raised his corpse from his grave and laid his body on the grass. I was right that his arms had been carved up as well.

Starting at both wrists there were four cut marks that crossed each other both horizontally and vertically forming a star. Below that one on his left arm there was a circle. There was an arrow pointing at the star while another line pointed another direction but was finished with a sideways dash. The symbols on his right arm following the star looked like a slanted three with the final bit stretching down a fair bit longer. The last symbol looked like a square without the bottom line.

Instead, that line looked like it cut through the image.

After looking at Ethan's body the cause of his death was rather obvious to tell. The dried blood around the shirt drew attention to it. Whoever had killed Ethan Shaw had stabbed him through his chest all the way into his heart.

Worse than all of that however was the residue of dark magic that radiated off of the spot where Ethan got stabbed. It sent a shiver down my spine. Whatever weapon made that injury was clearly cursed. Going by the feeling the dark magic gave me, it was probably accurate to say that this was not the first person's life it had taken away.

"Freeze!" a voice shouted from behind me.

Dealing with that problem wasn't bad enough because while I was dealing with the revelation about Ethan, I had lost focus on what was going on around me.

The fact that Northwood Park was near a school, a playground, and a neighborhood was something I had been aware of, but I had ignored the fact of what would happen when the people who lived and worked near here saw a stranger digging holes in the park.

Someone eventually decided to contact the police and report on my actions.

Added in with the fact that I was standing in front of a hole with a dead body and a dirty shovel it could be assumed that I was up to no good and should be treated dangerously.

That's why when I raised my head and turned around, I found a gun pointed at me by a male police officer.

"Put your hands up!" The officer shouted.

I could have chosen to be difficult. Tell him that those were rather contradictory orders, but I knew that there was no way I could reasonably talk my way out of this mess. So, I decided to comply with his demands and raised my hands. If I resisted this, then I would look guilty and probably be subjected to a manhunt by the police.

That would make solving Ethan's murder rather complicated.

Having seen that I was not going to struggle or try to run the officer put me in handcuffs and read me my rights as he put me in the back of his squad car. I watched through the window as the officer called for backup and told them about Ethan.

This situation was a minor hiccup when compared to everything else.

The officer drove me to the twenty-fourth district precinct. It was the closest police station to Northwood Park so arriving didn't take that long and it took even less time to get me secured in an interrogation room.

They chained my handcuffs to the table and left me with only silence and my thoughts for company. They were probably watching me on the other side of the mirror and searching for who I was.

The only thing I could do at the moment was sit and wait to tell the detectives my side of the story.

While they were waiting for whatever they were waiting for I went over everything I knew about this case, and I had to admit that it wasn't a lot. I had gotten a little bit of information and went off on like nothing else mattered. With magic I could skip over all the pointless work that detectives spent their time wasting on asking people who wouldn't answer questions.

The thing about that was in that type of situation besides the aunt I had no people who I could use to convince the detectives that I was innocent.

I made no connections with the people in Ethan's life and now that it was important to prove my innocence, I had nothing. I had treated this as a missing person case, and I was right given that he was missing.

However, without the knowledge that he was dead all that did was push me more and more into the guilty category.

As the seconds passed, I went over ideas on how to get out of this building and get back on the case. The first few were ignored as they involved violence and that wasn't in the cards because of the whole manhunt thing I was trying to avoid.

The twelfth idea, however, seemed good. The reason being that I hadn't even need to use any noticeable magic. No need for wall-breaking explosions, giant fireballs, or strikes of lightning that would make me seem like a supervillain.

While magic was usually about spells and rituals there are plenty of abilities that you could learn if you were dedicated enough, or your teacher was an insane taskmaster. I had both the determination and the annoying teacher.

Astral Projection was an ability that while I usually used for fun would serve me really well right now. With it I could travel anywhere in the blink of an eye and my physical body wouldn't move an inch.

Moving back in my chair I took a deep breath. I placed my hands on the table, and I began to concentrate on the place that I wanted to go. I just had to hope that Marcus was in town and at his mansion because with him it wasn't always a sure thing. Otherwise, I would have to come up with another idea.

After finding him it then took fifteen minutes or so to get everything set up. With that done I laid my head down and tried to go to sleep.

I was guaranteed to get out of here now and I was going to be very busy so it might do me some good to try and regain the magic that I had spent. I pulled my chair back, put my head on my handcuffed hands and closed my eyes.

My eyes opened when I heard the door opened.

I groaned as it felt like I had only slept ten minutes but the thing with dreams is you can't tell how long time has been moving so I had no clue how long I had truly been asleep. The room I was held in had no clock.

Two detectives walked in. Their badges shining on their belts, it was a man and a woman different as could be.

The man had short black hair with white on the edges and grey eyes. He was wearing a black tie and suit, and he had a folder with him.

If I am honest, he looked like a skinnier and older version of Brendan Fraser from the Mummy movies.

The woman on the other hand had dark orange hair that reached down to her shoulders, green eyes that looked similar to jade. Her suit was buttoned and completely blue, but you could see the black long sleeve shirt sleeves past the jacket.

She was the younger of the two and looked to be around my age give or take a year or two.

They introduced themselves and that is how I first met Detective Langdon and Detective O'Connell.

"Would you like to say anything before we begin scumbag?" Detective O'Connell asked me as he glared.

He was probably hoping that he could intimidate me into confessing and let them all go home.

They had probably learned that the officer that arrested me had read me my rights and given that I didn't call for a lawyer they probably assumed I was going to confess.

They were wrong in their assumption.

There were lessons that most children learn in their young life that are usable in certain circumstances even after they grow up. 'Deny, Deny, Deny,' was a phrase that was extremely useful right then.

The police will use tactics to try and convince people that it is in their best interests to talk to them. That they are on your side or that they can get you a better deal.

That is a lie.

In fact, until after the case of Miranda v. Arizona in nineteen-ninety-six the police did not even inform you that you could contact a lawyer to act on your behalf. They may have lost the case of Gideon v. Wainright in nineteen-sixty-three in which supreme court ruled that suspects in federal and state trials had the right to a lawyer but that did not mean that they gave up on trying to get easy confessions.

They would not get me that easily. They also had no concrete proof that I killed Ethan and wouldn't ever get any given that I had never met the kid until right before they arrested me. All the evidence they had of me could be explained away by a very good lawyer. Especially given the fact that my fingerprints weren't on the body.

"No not really. Though I would like to get out of these handcuffs." I answered them as I raised my hands.

"You have made your choice." Detective O'Connell said as he opened the folder.

"I will let you out as long as you do not try to hurt us or yourself." Detective Langdon said as she raised a key.

"You have a deal." I answered.

The first few seconds after the handcuffs were off, I just spent stretching my wrists.

"Enough. Now how about you explain this?" Detective O'Connell asked as he laid photographs of Ethan's corpse on the table.

They were probably expecting something in my eyes to show recognition of the body but there was nothing and they moved on.

"Ethan Shaw, eighteen-years-old, found dead with you standing over his body on top of a freshly dug hole what do you have to say to that?" Detective O'Connell asked with a hard look in his eyes.

Part of me wonders if this situation is karma for what I started and allowed to happen during my interrogation in the precinct. If so, then karma can just jump off a cliff. All those other criminals went on their way without suffering for their crimes, but I try and have some fun and I wind up close to death.

CHAPTER 5

The police had been busy while I schemed and slept. They had managed to discover Ethan's identity and have their medical examiner to take pictures of the corpse.

I just hoped they hadn't talked to the aunt yet. Learning that news without the proper context might cause her to form the wrong assumptions about what happened to her nephew.

I doubted that she would pay me if she thought I was the reason that her nephew was dead.

"That my metal detector needs to be repaired." I said.

I had been polite when talking with Susan, I kept silent during my arrest over Northwood Park, and I intended to keep silent until Marcus arrived but eventually that wall was going to come crumbling down and I would say something without thinking it through.

Especially when I was set up with a line like that.

Detective O'Connell didn't like that answer at all and he slammed his hands on the table shouting, "Do you think this is a joke? Some type of game?"

I fought the urge to have made a no game no life joke. I don't think he would have gotten the reference and first one aside I thought it might have been too soon to be making jokes out of Ethan's untimely demise.

The fact that Ethan died young is tragic, but I didn't like dwelling on emotions like that, so I buried them deep down inside of myself willing to ignore them whenever they showed up until they were gone. Talking about my feelings was not something I did with anyone.

Any therapist would say that was probably unhealthy, but it was how I coped with issues.

"No, I do not think it's a joke." I told them. "If I was making a joke, I would have asked you if your family was still fighting mummies or stealing diamonds with Daffy Duck and Bugs Bunny."

Detective O'Connell's eyes began to narrow at me.

I could see his face begin to twitch but I interrupted him before he could say anything.

"People have often told me I don't know when to stop talking. My teachers told me that I sometimes say the first thing that comes to my mind without thinking it through. That it would lead me to trouble. Maybe I should have taken their warnings more seriously. Still, you are fishing for information, but I unfortunately don't know what you want."

Detective Langdon feeling the rising tension in the room decided to intervene in the conversation.

"It doesn't look good for you." Detective Langdon said calmly. "You were found standing over the corpse in what looks to be a freshly dug grave."

She was right. Digging that hole without protection set in advance was reckless on my part.

"It is more than enough to have you charged with first degree murder and get you imprisoned for life." Detective O'Connell threatened with a glare.

"However, if you cooperate then we might be able to get you down to third degree murder." Detective Langdon said.

So, from what they believed to be my natural lifespan to twenty to forty years.

If I had actually committed the murders, then I might have been worried. At the time I was more amused that I was facing the good cop/bad cop routine. I had seen it on television plenty of times but this was the first time that i experience it in person.

Detective Langdon was the kind cop. The one who made you think she was understanding you while Detective O'Connell was there to be the rough and angry detective who looked like he would love nothing more than to beat the answers out of you.

I wondered how used to this style they were. It may have been their true personalities, but you could never be sure.

"It might look that way but there is a perfectly rational explanation that will prove my innocence." I said grateful that my hands were free.

It would be rather hard to make hand gestures if they were leashed to the table. Also, it would allow me to move on to the next part of my plan.

"Oh really, I would love to hear it. What possible explanation could you possibly give?" Detective O'Connell asked with suspicion in his voice.

Any sign of joy was smothered. Like most performances my plan would require help from my audience and Detective O'Connell played his part wonderfully.

"I am going to reach in my pocket for my business card." I said.

I wanted to make sure they had no reason to think I would pull a weapon out on them. They might get anxious and try to restrain me to the table in the belief that I was going to try and take them hostage. My reaction to that would not be pleasant and the violence that followed would be counterproductive.

My hands were clapped together and then I turned and slid them so that they were lying atop each other and then slowly put them back in a clapped formation. As my hands separated a card was revealed between them.

The card was placed on the table.

It was purple, on the back was a picture of an open eye in black ink with my number on it. On the other side was my business information. I already knew what it said, so I gave it to them to look over.

Alex Blackwell – Psychic Detective

Investigations, Charms, Séances, Item Recovery, Exorcisms, Fortune Telling, Mind Reading, Aura Reading, Bounty Hunter, Consulting, Reasonable rates.

When I started my business, I wondered how I would get people to contact me and so using magic on the cards made sense at the time. They were enchanted to appear throughout the city before those with problems.

Beyond the general spell summoning that witches and wizards learned eventually they would go to focus on their focused and trained in what they were interested in or naturally skilled at. Enchanting was my specialty. I had talents in other fields, but enchanting was the skill that I was the best at.

Enchanting is the art of infusing magic into physical items and giving them desired abilities. Cards like these are probably how Susan had found me.

The slight problem with these cards was that they did not disappear after the person called me. At the time of the enchantment, it had not been a concern of mine. That fault led to more people finding out about me, but it also led to prank calls to my office.

"Psychic, is that the answer you're going with?" Detective O'Connell questioned as he held the card in his hand.

"Yes, it is true after all." I answered. "I had been hired to find Ethan Shaw and a vision led me to the park. I had no idea why I needed to bring the shovel, but I listened to the vision and took one. I was rather disturbed when I figured out what the vision meant."

This world's science couldn't prove me wrong as far as I knew. The fact of the matter was the only reason psychics were doubted was because people grew more cynical as they aged. The sense of wonder and mystery of the world they had as children shattered as they conformed with society's beliefs.

"What like that show Psych?" Detective Langdon said somewhere between mockery and concern.

I paused for a few seconds to let the tension build before I turned towards her giving a sigh that tried to sound incredibly insulted and depressed. "I get asked that question so many times. No, I am a real psychic detective."

On the inside though I one day hope to be able to be as convincing as Shawn Spencer when convincing people that I was psychic. His acting skills were far beyond mine. I still had trouble portraying emotions on demand that I actually felt.

"Unless you are pleading an insanity defense, I don't think anybody will buy that." Detective O'Connell said as he tossed my card back to the table.

"That is rude." I said scowling as I moved to take my card back. "Don't you policemen have to do sensitivity training or something?"

"So, Alex, you think you are psychic?" Detective Langdon asked.

I could tell she was trying to humor me. She might have believed that I was playing crazy and wanted to see just how deep I would go in the act.

"Come on Langdon he's clearly a few colors short of a crayon box." Detective O'Connell said talking like I wasn't here.

If he was to be compared with the police academy characters, he would be lieutenant Harris.

"Watch and I'll prove it." I said as I pushed my shoulders back and got relaxed in the metal chair in the room.

The two detectives kept their eyes on me, but I wasn't sure if anybody else was watching us since the window I was facing was only one way. It allowed others to see me but not the reverse.

"How's that?" Detective O'Connell asked.

"I will tell you your future." I responded.

That brought a raised eyebrow and a doubtful expression from the detective.

All of this was part of my effort to stall for time. I didn't have the ability to look into the future and I was glad. Books always claim that being able to see the future meant that life had no surprises anymore. That when you saw all the good things that life could bring you would find yourself bored and disappointed.

I was not sure about that, but the lack of ability didn't stop me from making something up. Especially if I knew that it would be coming true soon enough.

"Oh yeah? Well go on and tell me." Detective O'Connell said in response.

I turned my full attention to Detective O'Connell and tried to ignore Detective Langdon's presence for the moment.

He was probably hoping that if he got me nervous enough that I might make a mistake that he and his partner could take advantage of. That wasn't going to happen. Not even on his best day. I had been trained to run circles around people like him and I will admit at the time a part of me enjoyed it. It wasn't because he was a cop or because I didn't like him.

The reason I was doing this was simple. It seemed like fun at the time.

"Hold out your hand." I said holding out mine.

"I am not holding your hand." Detective O'Connell said scowling.

"Then just hold out your palm. It is all I need." I said with a smile.

Detective O'Connell kept his scowl but opened his palm.

"I see you full of anger and at the sight of me getting out of here completely innocent." I told him.

I wished that I had some tarot cards just to make it more mysterious but one business card they missed in a search was one thing. Pulling an entire deck of cards would be a bit harder for them to explain to themselves.

"Really now?" Detective O'Connell interrupted me. "Because what I see for you is life with no chance of parole involved in it."

His expression at the time was a deep scowl that just seemed like its purpose was to radiate anger and fear and cause suspects to become scared. He was turning into a black hole trying to suck all the joy out of me and leave me a shattered husk full of angst and regret.

I wondered if he practiced the look in front of children and small animals and grew satisfied when they tried to escape from his gaze.

My unfazed reaction at his intimidation seemed to make Detective O'Connell eyes to light up with anger.

"It looks like my prediction is going to be proven true." I mumbled just loud enough for him to hear. Hearing that caused his fingers to tense. His chains of self-control were snapping.

This was a result of working in their world. It was a world of grey that just had lighter and darker shades. I on the other hand worked in a world of color. There were reds, blues, greens, and yellows. My world is like a kaleidoscope. You could spend hours looking at the colors and still find new combinations.

"This is ridiculous." Detective O'Connell as he gave up on trying to intimidate me.

"I can only work with what I see." I said.

"Let's try and move back to the interrogation." Detective Langdon said.

"What do you wish to know?" I asked turning to her.

I wondered how far we could get before Marcus got here.

"What I would like to be told is why this kid had to die!" Detective O'Connell shouted at me with his index finger pointed at me.

His face had turned deep red like a tomato and on his forehead one of his veins had started to throb.

That must have been painful. When I watched cartoons, I always wondered how angry people must be to become like that and how much it hurt.

"I must admit that I don't know the answer to your questions detective. However, when I find the killer, I will ask him for you." I told him point blank.

That would be my next move the moment that I left the precinct.

"I already found him and I'm looking right at him." Detective O'Connell said.

"Really?" I asked as I turned to look around before turning back to him. "I didn't know that you could see invisible people."

"What?" Detective O'Connell asked.

"I mean I don't see a guy in here besides you and me in this room and I know I didn't do it. In fact, keeping me held in here with a killer in the room seems like rather poor treatment of a tax paying citizen."

Detective O'Connell was about to say something else but there was a knock at the door interrupting him.

We all turned to face the door.

"Come in." Detective O'Connell said with a sigh of frustration. The next moment two people walked into the room.

The man on the left looked to be in charge. He had a fat face with black hair and hazel eyes. He had mutton chops stretched past his ears and reached to the middle of his face, his mustache stretched from his nose and covered his top lip but was parted down the middle like a greater or less than sign but going down.

This was the police captain of the precinct Bennett.

The man standing next to him would be my way out of this room.

Marcus was taller than me standing at a good six foot three with short dark hair and brown eyes, He looked to be twenty-five, He had a dark suit with a silver watch on his wrist and had a brown briefcase when he walked in. His black shoes were shiny yet barely made a sound when he walked. In his right hand he was wearing a ring on his middle finger. It was silver on the outside and on the inside was a red gem.

It was one of my better enchantments in my opinion.

I will admit when I told him to look like a lawyer when he picked me up, I did not expect that he would actually go this far as I knew that he did not own suits. A part of me wondered where he got it from and what happened to its original owner.

"Captain what is going on?" Detective Langdon asked as she rose from the table and looked at the two men.

"Apparently this is Marcus Johnson. He is the lawyer for your suspect." Captain Bennett said. "You are to release your suspect into this man's custody."

I nodded and began getting up out of the chair. I loved it when my plans actually worked right. I should have taken that as a sign then that my problems were only going to get worse.

"Wait, wait, wait." Detective O'Connell said as he rose to his feet. "If you are his lawyer, how did you even know that he was here? He has not made any phone calls since he was arrested."

For all of Detective O'Connell's issues you could not say that he was not a good detective.

I assume he was thinking that we were accomplices for the murder and that he had watched as I was driven away in a police car. However, I, had planned for this event when I told him to come.

"I texted him while I was in the police car. The arresting officer was so busy calling in for backup that he stopped paying attention to me." I said. "Unfortunately, I had to leave the phone in the car when I was taken out. I would like it back before I leave."

Just another detail to help sell the story. None of that was true but if called on it I would make sure that when I walked to the car, I would pull out my cell phone that could be reached through my coat pocket. They might want to check the phone for the text messages, but I could deny that. The sight of the phone was enough to corroborate my story.

CHAPTER 6

So, after Captain Bennett had let me leave the interrogation room, I took a look around the police station. The place looked like it was taken from a television set. There were people typing on computers, officers eating donuts at the break table, and officers writing up reports from people sitting in chairs next to the desk.

None of them paid a single bit of attention to us.

I turned when I heard footsteps behind me. It seems that the detectives were not happy about me being released.

"Captain why are you letting him go?" Detective Langdon asked.

A part of me felt sympathetic to the detectives. No amount of their logical questions or their reasonable suspicions would get the detectives an answer that they would like. Marcus left little to no loopholes in his work.

A situation like that would drive me mad.

"The evidence we have over him is circumstantial at best." Captain Bennett said.

It seems that was the final note for the control Detective O'Connell self-control.

"Circumstantial? We have him standing beside a corpse with a shovel and a deep hole dug in the ground!" Detective O'Connell shouted as he walked up to his captain.

At the time had I wanted to taunt him further I would have reminded him of my prediction when I was being interrogated.

"I would like to state for the group that I found the bodies through psychic means." I broke into the conversation. "My only crime was digging it up."

The glare that he sent back at me had so much heat I bet he could have boiled eggs with it.

I turned to look back around the precinct and saw that there was no reaction to Detective O'Connell's arguments. The officers just kept typing on their computers.

I wondered if they were used to O'Connell shouting in the office.

"Yes circumstantial." Captain Bennett said.

Marcus clapped his hands together gaining everyone's attention.

"Now I want to you to go away and if there are any recordings of my client's interrogation, after you have finished that I want you to return to your office because I have something else that I want you to do for me." Marcus said.

This saved so much time and effort I am glad I didn't decide to go with the fighting my way-out plan.

"Yes, I will." The captain said in a daze and walked away.

"What are you doing?" Detective O'Connell questioned shouting at his captain.

He did not understand that his captain had little to no free will at the moment. Captain Bennett had made eye contact with Marcus earlier and that had been a horrible mistake. Eye contact is the only thing a vampire needed to turn a person into a puppet.

"You don't have time to worry about him." Marcus said looking at the detectives.

"What did you just do?" Detective Langdon asked and Detective O'Connell drew his gun.

The next second after that happened Marcus turned into a blur. I turned my head when I heard the thud of detective Langdon as he landed on the ground grunting in pain.

When nobody turned to look at the assaulted police officer, I realized what happened.

"If you want to follow his example, I can take your gun too." Marcus told Detective Langdon while putting the detective's gun on a desk.

It looked like she was going to listen and drop her gun so Marcus turned around but before he could take a step she drew and shot him three times in the chest. Marcus only staggered backward but given that those bullets were made of silver and steel and not wood it was not a surprise that while it hurt him it wouldn't kill him.

Marcus spun back around facing her and looking like he would snap her neck.

Instead, he just sighed and took a deep breath to calm down before he focused on the detective. His brown eyes turned a crimson red.

Marcus's hypnotism could be used from a distance, but the control was not as good if he was not looking a person in the eyes.

"All right if you want to be that way, I order both of you to walk to the captain's office as well and don't leave or move a step until I tell you to." Marcus said as he pointed to a room with the blinds drawn down.

They nodded no longer in control of their bodies, and Detective Langdon pulled O'Connell up and they walked there together.

"What took you so long?" I asked him even though I had yet to learn what time it was.

"First I had to find a suit that made it seem like I was actually a lawyer. Then I had to meet the captain and put him under my control. Finally, I had to hypnotize all the officers in this precinct." Marcus said as he listed off with his fingers.

"How did you get the suit?" I questioned as I ran my fingers through my hair. I hoped he took it from a department store.

"It took a while to find a guy who wore a suit that was in my size and then I had to follow him to his place and see what suit I would like best." Marcus answered.

I sighed at his reasoning.

"You know that I am really picky about what I wear." Marcus defended his actions.

"Should I be worried for the guy that you stole the suit from?" I asked.

Unless his target was really lucky no human could possibly fight Marcus, he was supernaturally fast and strong and when you throw in hypnotism there should be no person capable of causing him trouble.

"No, it's fine. He believes that he decided to be charitable and donate a few of his suits to a man that could appreciate them." Marcus answered.

"Why did you do all of this extra work?" I asked as I gestured to the officers around the room.

There was the temptation to start poking people with a stick and seeing what it would take to make them react.

"I figured that it would be useful for me to have police officers on hand if I ever need them." Marcus said.

"You plan to keep them under your control?" I asked. That had not been part of the plan.

"There are situations where I might need them." Marcus said.

I felt bad about what might happen, but I decided to move on. Complaining about his mind control would have been hypocritical when my plan on leaving that interrogation room relied on him using his gifts.

"Alright then. Let's finish up with this and head out." I said as I walked to the captain's room with Marcus following behind me.

Walking in the room I saw the two of them standing still and not moving. It was creepy, the only thing they were doing besides breathing was staring off into nothing.

Marcus took the captain's seat and began spinning around enjoying the chair's wheels.

"All right now you can wake up but don't move from where you are." Marcus told them.

I could have left but I wanted to make sure Marcus didn't do anything too damaging to the officers. The best outcome I hoped for was that he would only erase the memories of the detectives from the moment where they walked into the interrogation room.

I watched as their eyes became focused and they realized where they were.

"What is going on?" Detective O'Connell asked.

"Well, you and your partner decided to shoot a vampire and the result wasn't in your favor." I told them while leaning on the door.

"Vampire?" Detective O'Connell asked with scorn.

With that opening cue Marcus stopped spinning and stared at the detective.

"Yes, and before you make a twilight joke know I can and will make your life a thing of eternal misery and unending torture." He said tapping the desk.

I winced at the things he could come up when he was truly motivated to cause someone pain.

"You are just as insane as your friend I don't know what drug you put me, my partner, and the captain on but be sure I will make sure you both end up in an insane asylum." Detective O'Connell declared.

The next time we met he would not remember any of this.

Marcus didn't say anything. He just tapped the captain's desk for a few seconds while tilting his head.

After the third tilt he stood up and revealed his vampire face. The face that vampires had when they were going to bite someone. It was like his regular face except his brown eyes turned red again, his veins were more obvious, and his canine teeth extended into fangs.

All I heard was a whoosh sound and the next thing I saw was Marcus holding the detective several feet off the ground with one hand around his throat.

Marcus tossed him into a wall and watched him fall to the ground before he turned to Detective Langdon.

"Do you have any doubts about what I am now?" Marcus asked as his face returned to normal again.

Detective Langdon made a smart decision and shook her head side to side.

I guess she didn't feel like crashing into the wall like her partner.

I saw his suit and saw where she had shot him, and it looked like those bullets earlier had pierced his chest and so I came into the conversation.

Not because I was concerned but more because I was curious about something.

"She shot you through the heart?" I asked him and I wondered if she knew Bon Jovi's song and how she felt about the idea of love.

"Yeah, can you believe it I was all nice and when I turn my back, she shot me?" He asked sounding so offended at what happened.

I couldn't help but laugh at the time.

We had no clue that it wouldn't be the last injury his heart would take this week.

"Well, you did knock my partner down." She said gaining some resolve back into her voice.

She was lucky that it was Marcus she was talking that way to as other vampires might not respond to that so well.

They were not known for being the most conversation friendly people.

"That is true, but it was still rude." Marcus countered like there was still some way that he was in the right.

"How did you do that?" Detective O'Connell asked as he began to get up and walked back over.

Guess he did not want to leave his partner alone with us.

"I gave you the answer already. I know the idea of an African American vampire is a rare thing but get it through your thick head." He said.

"No, I think he means how is it possible that Vampires are real?" Detective Langdon asked.

"Well, you know the saying that the good die young. What isn't told to people is that sometimes they come back." Marcus answered.

I could tell he had prepared that line in case anyone ever asked. Marcus spent a lot of time coming up with what he thought were cool one liners or clever phrases.

I did not judge him for it because I did it too.

If Marcus is to be believed he has been a vampire for six years. I had known him for half of that time. I wasn't told the reason that he was turned but I knew Marcus wasn't busy hunting down the person who turned him so that ruled out reasons like love or hate.

He enjoyed being a mystery and I didn't care enough to push the issue.

"How do you become a vampire?" Detective Langdon asked.

"It's an intense process. As you die you feel as if you have been brought to the edge of a cliff. Each second you feel as if the path behind you has grown darker and then you when you wake feel the urge to complete the process. Feeling as if you have been walking through a desert for days without water. Then you have your first taste of blood." Marcus began.

Listening as he began to monologue; I realized that I would have to move things along.

"Oh, it's simple. It follows vampire diaries rules. You die with vampire blood in you and then when you come back you drink human blood." I said.

Marcus glared at me, but I rolled my eyes at him and gestured for him to hurry up. The door turned and the captain walked in.

"I have done as you wished." Captain Bennett said.

"So, if he's a vampire what are you?" Detective O'Connell asked me.

"I am a wizard." I told him and pulled my wand from my coat.

"I can't believe I am being held hostage by a vampire and a discount Harry Potter." Detective O'Connell said scowling.

I felt my eye twitch.

Marcus was no help at the time, he was just laughing and moved back to the desk he was borrowing.

"He's got you there." Marcus said.

I truly felt like cursing him there, but he was still needed so I picked a different target.

"Leave if you want." I told Detective O'Connell and watched as he tried only to remember that he was stuck here because Marcus hadn't told him he could leave and when he glared at me.

"Alright I'm bored now." Marcus said. "Time to finish this."

"Then hurry up." I said nonchalantly as I walked to the wall to hide a concerned glance at Marcus.

While we were friends, I couldn't trust their safety with him alone as the role model Marcus had for his life was Lestat de Lioncourt and that made him unpredictable. Marcus is a vampire who was always searching for something to excite him.

That meant that his impulse control varied depending on his mood and the goal he was aiming for.

Despite my reservations I contacted Marcus because while he was all for being fun and reckless, he was also paranoid of what would happen if people found out he was a vampire. I knew he wasn't fond of the idea of people hunting him down for revenge or hate like Frankenstein's monster or because he killed somebody they knew, or they had a problem with vampires. It was why he didn't drink blood from the neck and tried really hard not to kill people.

He still drank human blood it was just that the people he drank from were hypnotized into putting the blood into bags for him. He stored them in a fridge in his mansion.

I watched as Marcus picked Detective O'Connell up again and made sure that they were looking at each other straight in the eyes and he began to hypnotize him again.

The detective's face was full of fear and anger. He was probably imagining what would happen to him and his partner.

Detective Langdon tried to intervene. She broke free of the hypnotism and was about to draw another gun from her ankle but given that we were close by and the fact that I didn't want tinnitus I had to intervene.

I spun my wand in my hand and pointed at her.

"Lignum Ligaveris." I said and the wood rose up from the floor and wrapped itself around her not allowing her to fire her gun due to the fact the only person she would be shooting is herself.

"You are going to go home and forget you ever arrested him. You will believe that Alex is just a psychic detective helping you as a consultant on the case and you will not remember anything about what we talked about in this room." Marcus told them.

Thankfully it seemed that Marcus was not in the mood to drive them to a mental breakdown. After Marcus finished with the detectives he turned to the captain.

I released Detective Langdon and we left before they came back to consciousness.

CHAPTER 7

After I walked outside the building the first thing I did was look up into the sky and just gaze at the moon. Besides the streetlights that illuminated the path it was the hugest source of light at the moment.

There were no stars due to the city lights and the so the only things blinking in the sky were either radio towers or airplanes.

The wind might have been cold for other people but thanks to my coat I never felt it. The coat was layered with enchantments. From simple ones that either kept me warm or cold depending on the weather to complex ones like my pockets which had infinite space.

I gave a yawn. I had been in that building way too long and I had yet to go back and retrieve my car. It had been a long day, but I was nowhere near done.

"So, what are you going to do now?" Marcus asked as he stood on the sidewalk's edge and walked on top of it trying to keep perfect balance.

"I plan to get something to eat and then I will try and figure out who killed Ethan." I said.

The dominoes had been knocked over and I wanted to see the full picture.

Ethan had been killed with an object that was full of dark magic. That type of weapon could only be created by a someone who had fully intended to kill or injure someone. It was powered by death and its aim was to probably grow stronger to kill or hurt others.

The current belief regarding magic is that it contains three sides. There is a light side, a dark side, and a neutral side in-between that could be used to achieve a goal. All magic can be used to kill as magic could be used to help or to hurt depending on the person using it and their desires at the time.

It was there at the beginning of the universe before the first man stood on the planet and it would be the last spark to go out when the universe ended. Countless witches and wizards had spent their lives trying to understand this power.

Dark magic originated from the dark feelings that dwelt in the heart like anger, hatred, envy, and all the other emotions people feel when they want to kill a person and doing so only makes it stronger and easier to do it again.

It was drawn from darkness to spread darkness.

Light magic is what was created and generated by all the positive emotions created by beings in the world. It was still possible to kill with it if a person was clever enough.

Neutral magic came from a calm heart and mind.

There are many subcategories and styles that were developed from this belief.

I use natural magic. It is the practice of using the magic you were born with to create spells and potions. Each time you cast a spell you were using your own energy to cause something to happen. I preferred this method as it meant I depended on myself and my natural abilities.

No deals with duplicitous devils. No begging for favors from mercurial gods.

If death was what powered this cursed object than it was likely the killer is not going to be content with just Ethan. There were likely more dead bodies not found. Like Ethan they were probably buried in a way that prevented non-magicals from finding them or noticing that they had been buried there.

Whoever was behind this murder had to be stopped. However, the problem was that I had more questions and assumptions than facts. I had to figure out the method he was using to kill and the reasoning behind it.

According to his aunt Ethan Shaw looked to be a completely average kid. He was like any other high school kid. He went to school, got average grades, and liked to hang out with his friends afterwards at the mall.

None of that explained why he was killed and left buried in a park.

From the type of wound that I had seen on Ethan's corpse I can infer the weapon is a blade type. Either from a knife or a dagger. The magic that was used to kill Ethan looked to be more of a sacrificial type. The symbols on his arms and forehead could mean that it was part of a ritual. If that was true, then that meant the killer had to spend time with their victims in a place that they felt was safe and could be sure that no one would find them.

As I walked down the street, I held hope that whatever weapon that had been used in this murder had been forged long ago by some dark witch or wizard and lost to time. That the only reason this was happening was that some poor fool who did not know better happened to find it. Given an impulse that they could not ignore.

"Hello, are you listening?" Marcus asked.

That question brought me out of my daze, and I noticed that I had stopped right before I walked into his outstretched fist.

"What's the big idea?" I asked him.

"You were in your own world. I wondered if you would notice it, but you didn't so I had to warn you." Marcus said with a smile. "If you did not react after that well that would be your fault."

I glared at him which he just laughed at.

There were times I really found him annoying, but I figured if you have a friend that is an immortal that means you always have a friend you can use as a meat shield.

"So, what are you thinking so hard about?" Marcus asked.

"To get the information I want I have to ask someone that had been involved in the event." I said.

"That would be useful but how do you plan to do that?" Marcus asked. "The only one we know for sure that is still alive is the killer. Which kinds of hinders your ability to find someone to ask about the killer."

"It is simple. I am going to summon Ethan's spirit." I told him.

The thing most people believed but did not really know is that when people died, they all had an afterlife. Whatever religion you followed there was a god and heaven, hell, or whatever to go to. It was one of the deals that was made with the gods when they left this world for the others.

Whenever anyone died, they would go to the Final Station before being sent to the afterlife of whatever god or gods they followed.

I believed that Ethan could hold some of the answers that I was looking for and could help make this mystery simple.

"Do you need help with anything?" Marcus asked.

I shook my head and pulled out my phone. "I have everything that I need in my workshop. I am going to need you to check up on Ethan's aunt and make sure she is okay."

"Sure. No problem." Marcus said as he brought out his flip phone. "I will check it out in the morning."

I watched him walk off the street sidewalk a care.

A car was driving up and it stopped just before it hit what they must have assumed was a crazy person standing in the street.

"Move out of the way!" The driver shouted while honking his horn three times.

His face was tense and annoyed. He looked like he was wanting to run Marcus over.

He probably should have driven around him because when Marcus walked up to him it was too late for him to run.

I could not hear what Marcus was saying but I knew what was happening. Marcus didn't like driving himself if he didn't have to. I knew that he had a driver's license and cars at his mansion. He just preferred forcing someone to do the driving for him.

Being a vampire was something that Marcus loved.

I could see why. He was immortal and could hypnotize his victims. He never had to work a day in his life if he did not want to.

If there wasn't the fact that I might lose my magic, I might have wanted to be a vampire.

I had planned to call him not long after I summoned Ethan. If I was fighting someone that was killing people in some strange ritual, then I might need backup that had supernatural strength and supernatural speed to help. I did not need him to suddenly vanish because he found something more interesting to do.

It turns out I shouldn't have asked because he wasn't much, and we didn't even get to the dark wizard yet.

I would have to get my car back first but after that it would be time to start a seance. There was too much distance between here and Northwood Park to simply walk just for my car and I was not in the mood to see if I was going to be robbed by walking alone at night.

So, I decided to use magic.

Teleportation is another magical ability like Astral projecting that I was taught that I was truly fond of. As a kid I didn't like walking long distances to accomplish those annoying tasks that my teacher gave me so when I learned that teleportation was an available skill, I put a lot of effort into figuring out how to do it.

Using magic to move from one place to another was simple, all you had to do was think of where you wanted to go and all you felt was yourself disappearing from one place and reappearing in another.

I had been working on that skill for years and so it only took five seconds to travel that distance.

CHAPTER 8

It was time to summon a spirit. An art that I had years of experience with.

I was deep in my workshop. Past the building and surrounded by an endless void of white. I didn't summon spirits outside my workshop due to the fact that there was always a chance they could escape but if they did so here all they would have is an endless void that they could not escape from.

When I first started learning magic summoning spirits back to this world had been my goal. I had lost my parents and wanted the chance to speak with them again.

The idea that I could call on them whenever times got difficult, or my lessons were particularly rough kept me focused.

I practiced so much that spirit summoning became my other specialty.

Looking down at the circle that was laying in front of me I glared and stretched out my hand trying to deal with the cramps that came along with drawing it.

I wasn't a fan of magic circles. Never had been and I don't think I ever will be. They were so complicated to draw. You had to be able to draw a perfect outer circle to start. Then you also had to be able to draw interior shapes to fit the circle perfectly. You had to worry about every single line because any smudge or line out of place and you would have to destroy the circle and star over from scratch.

Otherwise, you could have a very dangerous creature on the loose. If the summoner were skilled, they could subdue the summon before any serious damage was done. If not, then the best-case scenario is that their head is eaten quickly, and it is not their problem anymore.

My teacher told me plenty of such stories when I was learning.

I had no idea how Asian wizards and witches, anime characters, and their manga writers dealt with this.

My summoning circle was huge. It is full of runes, squares, triangles, and circles that overlap other circles that it hurt my eyes to just look at it and I was the person who drew it. The circle was meant to summon, bind, and control spirits.

This would probably be considered overkill by other wizards/ witches for a single summoning but being reckless when messing with spirits is a dangerous thing. If you aren't careful with spirits and the one, you want to summon is uncertain you might get the wrong one and then it decides that it will want to burn down your house or decide to haunt you for the rest of your life.

Just look at all the movies involving Ouija boards. Any time I got near one I burned it out of principle. I was having none of that.

In the center of the circle was another circle and inside that image there was another circle with a crescent moon inside which represented the sun and, in the circle, representing the sun there was the picture of Ethan that I was given.

To summon a spirit, you needed the name of the spirit, something that belonged to it, and something to bind it to.

Rule number one is to always be sure that you know who and what you are calling.

Spirits are the souls of people that are headed for their afterlife or reached it while ghosts are souls that remained on the earth because of lingering desires or resentments. Both kinds were categorized under books that involved doing séances.

I usually started with spirits then moved on to ghosts when I was summoning the deceased as spirits are calmer and more rational than ghosts. Less of a pain to deal with as well.

The more vengeful the ghost the harder it was to control and the more risk it had of breaking free.

Once a spirit is summoned in such a circle as this it is bound to the summoner by their mana and so each action they took and the longer they stayed around the more mana the summoner lost.

It didn't take much to summon Ethan and keep him bound to this world.

Focusing on the image of Ethan in my head and the picture in my hand, I began to chant. I didn't have my wand with me because I didn't need it for this. The purpose of my wand was to help me if I was in a fight that required spell casting but for things like enchanting or spirit summoning all I needed was focus.

"Si vocare spiritus." I chanted three times and watched as the circle began to light up and the image of Ethan began to appear before becoming a solid yet pale version of the kid in the picture.

I preferred this method of detective work even if creating the circle was a giant pain because who would be able to give me a better description of the killer than the victim. Medical examiners got their answers from the body, police officers from evidence, I just so happened to be able to call on the spirit of the victim to find the answers I needed.

I wasn't lying to the detectives when I said the spirits gave me the answer, I just wasn't using the correct tense in time.

Ethan eventually appeared out of nothing, but he looked better than his corpse.

As I looked over him when he had the ability to stand on his own, I realized that he was taller than his aunt Susan. He appeared wearing the clothes he had been wearing when he died but his skin lacked the marks his killer placed on him.

Unless he messed up by showing his supernatural abilities most non-magical people would not believe he was dead.

"What is going on?" Ethan asked disoriented and confused.

I however did not have the time for him to have an existential crisis.

"Ethan, I hate to be the one to inform you if no one else has yet but you're dead." I said to him.

It is my policy to be blunt and honest with ghosts and spirits. The types of spirits I deal with can usually talk on for hours at a time and I was in no mood for that today.

"What are you talking about?" Ethan questioned me.

He was clearly in the denial phase of death. He had died recently so maybe he had not been given a proper explanation. The afterlife was a busy place, and the paperwork probably did not help matters. It took people a while to recognize that they were dead. Usually, it was explained to them slowly and patiently, but I was too tired for that.

"You died. I believe that you were stabbed in the heart by a blade." I said to him trying to move the process along. "Do you know what it was?"

"You're insane!" He shouted at me.

He clearly was moving to the anger phase of being dead. If I could hurry this along and move him to acceptance, I was all for it. It was almost morning. I needed sleep and the sooner I got answers the sooner I could go to my bed.

"Ethan notice where you are and the fact that your feet aren't touching the ground." I said and gave a yawn and could feel my head pounding and my eyes beginning to strain to stay open.

It was a good thing that my workshop would allow me to my office.

He looked down and saw that he was floating a few inches above the ground and surrounded by a vast whiteness. When he landed, he tried to flee the circle and he soon regretted that decision because as soon as he tried leaving the circle with the moon and the sun he crashed into an invisible wall.

"What are you and what have you done to me?" He shouted at me clearly freaking out over what was happening to him.

He probably thought I kidnapped him and drugged him. I could have corrected him, but I wasn't in the mood. There was always time later to do so.

"I am a wizard, and I did nothing besides summoning you." I told him feeling like I was about to hit the ground at any moment. "Your Aunt Susan hired me to find you."

He tried leaving the circle again but only got more pain for his trouble.

"Don't try that again you can't escape." I warned him and watched as he began to bang on the wall with his fist trying to get out.

It was somewhat amusing, and it would have been funnier if he wasn't adding to my headache.

Having no other choice, I reached into my coat, which was now white like a cloud and pulled out a necklace. Both the string and the jewel on the end were black.

I pointed the necklace at Ethan who was still freaking out and annoying me.

This spirit binding necklace was something I enchanted to let me move and carry a spirit/ghost around. This way I wouldn't have to constantly destroy and recreate the summoning and binding circle.

It was connected to this room and the circle so if I wanted to get rid of the ghost all I would have to do is erase the circle on the necklace with magic and the same would happen to the circle in this space.

"Ligare Spiritus." I said and in he went screaming and I was finally given peace and quiet.

It looked like I would have to save the investigation for tomorrow but looking at the jewel in the necklace that now glowed white and had a copy of the magic circle on it I knew it would be a lot easier.

I headed over to the only building in my workshop and headed to the guest room that I had there and placed the necklace on the desk and went to sleep, not even changing my clothes as today was exhausting in ways that I didn't even know were possible.

With all the developments that happened today I was in no mood to be helping a spirit accept the fact that he was dead.

That would be the job for the me of tomorrow. This was the third mistake I had made.

I was fond of putting jobs off on the version of me that would have deal with it, and I truly regretted that habit right now and I wish I had given up on the case, but I didn't and so like Alice I would just be pulled deeper and deeper into wonderland.

CHAPTER 9

The night turned into day and after I had finished my breakfast, I decided that it was time to get back to work. That meant releasing Ethan and hoping that he had come to terms with what had happened to him.

"Absolvisti Spiritus." I said and Ethan came back out looking irritated and annoyed. "Are you ready to grant my three wishes?"

"Very funny." He said glaring at me. "Do you know how long I have been in there? Stuck in a cramped space with only my thoughts to pass the seconds?".

"I went through a lot yesterday and needed the rest." I told him unapologetically.

Saying that had really set him off.

"Well hooray for you." He sarcastically cheered with his hands moving for emphasis.

"Some people would pay good money to get away from the distractions of the city and focus deeper on themselves." I joked.

"All I gained is a deeper understanding of why people fear solitary confinement." Ethan said before frowning. "What do you want?"

Great. He was ready to help. Or too depressed to argue. Either was fine with me but I chose to believe that it was the first.

"What I want is information on the person that killed you." I told him. "Anything that can give me a clue on how to find him or how he found you."

I had promised to tell the detectives earlier that I would tell them when I found the answer and I always strove to be helpful in my own way.

"You want information?" Ethan asked me with his tone growing with in annoyance. "Do you think we had a nice introduction with cookies and tea where he explained his reasoning before he decided to carve through my skin and kill me with that weird knife of his?"

His feet began to lightly lift off of the ground though I doubt that he noticed.

Since I wasn't a fan of teen angst, I focused on the knife part. While I did not expect Tolkien level descriptions, I was hoping for something that would help me.

"Your decision to be sarcastic is not helpful in any way." I told him.

"Well, I am sorry." Ethan complained. "The killer was wearing a mask that prevented me from seeing his face."

Of course, he had to be wearing a mask. I could have used the police and their resources to search through the city if Ethan had known what his killer looked like. The universe seemed to just love making this case harder for me.

I did not know how right I was.

"So magic is real?" Ethan questioned me looking curious.

"Yes, given the fact that you spent a night in a necklace should be enough to prove that magic is real." I said rubbing my hand through my hair.

I had to hope that he had some kind of clue that could help me.

"Well, if magic is real how come the world doesn't know?" He asked me as he let his feet touch the ground though I doubt he noticed.

"Because we work really hard to keep it a secret." I said. "When the pantheons were leaving this world for their own many magical creatures and beings followed after them. That made it easy for magic to be hidden due to the fact that countless magical races were gone. The ones that stayed behind looked enough like the people of this world to blend in, small enough that it was hard to see them, or held a special ability that made them easy to ignore. My government has entire departments that are focused on preventing such exposure."

The methods that they are willing to go to keep the secret were the stuff of nightmares.

"Why?" He asked. "You could help a lot of people with magic. All the diseases that people suffer and the tragedies they experienced could be prevented with a simple spell."

He was likely thinking if people were more aware of magic he wouldn't have died.

"It is true that magic probably could help a lot of people but there were also lots of problems that would be created if magic was revealed to the world." I told him.

In my opinion revealing magic to the world ended in two ways. One we rule the world or two we are experimented on so everyone can have magic. Neither of those option sounded good to me because eventually each would lead to a war that would kill a lot of people.

I had read books where such occasions happened and did not want to live in a world like that.

Anyway, it was time to get back to the reason that I had summoned him. The fact that he could help me solve his murder and find the dark wizard behind it.

"What did the weapon look like?" I asked him.

"It was sharp, and it hurt." He said bluntly.

"Can you give me more than that?" I asked him. "That description would have me search every house inside the city."

He again did not take my opinion very well.

"Hey, I'm trying to remember but the pain is the thing I remember most." He said looking away.

I nodded, giving in and signaling him to continue.

"The blade itself was about four inches I guess, and it was a strange black color, and it had a brown handle and there were symbols on it." He said gripping his arm.

I wrote that down to make sure I knew what I was looking for.

"How did he find you?" I asked trying to understand why Ethan was picked. "Were you patrolling through the night looking for criminals to fight?"

"What are you talking about?" He asked. "He did not say why he was cutting into me, but he said something about being grateful for my sacrifice and he would put it to good use."

I nodded writing down his answer. It could have all been by chance. That he wanted victims that were young. Ethan's death could just be the result of having the worst luck in the world.

"Do you know where he took you?" I asked him.

"I believe that it was a warehouse." He said.

"Can you be more specific than that?" I asked him. "What kind of supplies were around you?"

"I could only see the wall and the backdoor to the ocean briefly." He said. "He moved me to a table where I could only see the ceiling. Whatever he had me under made it impossible for me to move."

"It was most likely a paralysis spell." I said.

This killer certainly was sadistic. Keeping him aware enough to be able to feel pain but not able to move or run.

"Alright I will keep all of this in mind during the search." I said. "Let us just hope that he uses that place for all of his murders."

"So now that you have what you need, I guess that you are going to send me back to my afterlife?" Ethan asked with a sigh.

"Not yet." I said. "How would you feel if I kept you around for this case?"

"Why would you do that?" Ethan asked surprised.

"I figured that you would be able to enjoy your afterlife more if you knew that your killer had been captured and was awaiting trial." I answered.

"What do you get out of it?" Ethan asked with a suspicious tone.

"Do you have trouble believing that I feel your death was a tragedy and that you deserve justice?" I asked. "That I can tell your Aunt Susan that you had found peace? There is plenty of injustice in the world. Is it so strange that I might want to add a dash of kindness and compassion where I could."

"I would like to believe that, but I still have the feeling that there is something in this for you." Ethan said.

I wonder if I would need acting classes to truly convince people that I wanted to help?

"There is also the fact that I would get paid for catching a dark Wizard." I said to convince him. "Good thing too as I doubt that I would get the rest of the money from your aunt."

If he was looking for a suspicious reasoning, then greed would be good enough.

"Alright I will stay and help." Ethan agreed now that he believed he knew my motivation to be self- serving.

"Great." I said bringing the necklace back out and watched as he was sucked right back in.

If I had instead decided to beat up my conscience instead of listening to it, then I wouldn't be in my current mess. The fact that I cared too much was a major factor of how I ended up about to be killed by a vampire.

Going to my desk and grabbing a map of the city I tried scrying again this time for signs of dark magic that was similar to the remnants on Ethan's body, and I used the necklace as the crystal using the connection between his spirit, his body, and the ritual to find what I was looking for.

I marked five spots on the map where the necklace fell down with an x. Looking down at the map and ignoring the one where I found Ethan's body, I saw that there were only four spots in the city that had the same trace of magic.

One of those spots held warehouses and was near water.

Given what I already knew from Ethan I decided to head there first. I was going to have to check out all of these places eventually but definitely the warehouse area first as that might be the location that Ethan had been murdered in.

I grabbed the map and a satchel and left the workshop. After looking online, I had the general area and an image of the warehouses. I was ready to go and teleported to the nearest street.

When I arrived at the warehouse location a new problem appeared. The only thing I saw was an empty field barred by a barbed wire gate. There was a large mass of water beyond the land but no warehouse.

This time I kept faith in my skills and did not doubt that the warehouse was here. That could only mean that the warehouse had been cloaked to prevent people from seeing that it was there. It was possible that the warehouse in question was more than likely abandoned a while ago but still to have an entire building go missing and have no one question it.

I really had to be amazed at the skill involved and the lack of attention people pay to things in these modern times.

As I walked closer to the fence, I could feel that a slight suggestion entered my mind to tell me to ignore this place and move on.

I ignored that suggestion and glared at the space.

So, it was less a matter of ignorance and more that people's mind being altered when they tried to stare at the space where the warehouse was. That was probably why nobody had seriously checked this place out.

Not the elderly who should have remembered an abandoned warehouse, the adults that worked in such a place or the kids who should have wanted to climb this fence and play in what looked to be an empty field.

I brought out the necklace and released Ethan.

"Why have you brought me to an empty field?" Ethan asked as he looked past the fence.

"I believe that this is the place that you were killed." I answered calmly while wondering what to do. "The warehouse is hidden by a spell."

Unravelling the cloaking spell would be pretty easy but if I did it now, that would lead to problems. So, I would have to make sure all the people living and working nearby didn't decide to investigate the case of the mysteriously returning abandoned warehouse.

The solution to my problem came quickly.

After all what was the point in having a mind controlling vampire on speed dial that owes you favors if not to cash in on them?

Reaching into my coat and pulling out my cell phone I called Marcus. I could have done it myself, but vampire hypnotism was stronger than my compulsion charms. My phone is a Metro pcs android. It had trouble holding a charge at times, but I didn't like change and was very stubborn, so I kept it despite the headaches that it gave me.

Part of it is due to the way it looked in its red and black case.

It only took two rings before he answered, and I could tell he wasn't happy that I was calling him in for another job.

"Alex, I have got bad news for you." He said.

"What has happened?" I asked wondering what new complication the world wanted to throw at me.

"I walked in the house uninvited, and the aunt isn't here." He said.

I nodded along until what that meant caught up with me and I froze.

The thing about vampires being unable to walk inside a house they hadn't been invited inside is true. Unless the owner was dead or sold the property and I did not believe in the second option that much.

"Was there a chance that she had been renting the house?" I asked him after I had walked some distance away from Ethan.

"That could be possible." Marcus said. "Did she seem that she was planning to go on a trip?"

"With her nephew missing I doubt it." I said before shaking my head. "We'll deal with that later just come down here I need your help."

The irony of the situation tempted me to laugh. I had been hired to find a missing nephew and now I had to tell the nephew that his aunt had gone missing.

I hated how such a simple case decided to take a swan dive into a pool of insanity.

Looking at the events from my current location I wish that I had backed out and buried my head in the sand.

It took about fifty minutes for Marcus to arrive, and he was wearing a different black suit from the one he picked me up from the police station in. He walked up to us with the stride of a man who had no problems in life.

"What kind of help did you need?" Marcus asked, looking at the field.

"The killer has hidden this warehouse on the other side of this fence. We have to cross it and find out what he is doing in there." I said. "I called you in case people come out of their houses and start asking questions."

Then it was time to introduce the two to each other.

CHAPTER 10

"This is Marcus. He's a friend of mine." I told Ethan then turned to Marcus. "Marcus this is Ethan the spirit I told you that I planned to summon to help with this case."

"Impressive work. If I did not know he was dead, then I would assume that he is just another person." Marcus said as he walked around Ethan in a circle.

I watched as Marcus clearly not knowing the difference between a ghost and a spirit tried to put his hand through Ethan to see if he could put it right through him. He was surprised when his hand failed to pass through him and just touched his shirt.

"Woah back up!" Ethan cried as he jumped away from Marcus.

"Shouldn't I have phased through him?" Marcus asked me.

I shook my head. "That is for ghosts. You aren't able to touch them, and they can't touch anything else. You can touch spirits."

It was part of what increased their resentment and their aggression. The fact that they could watch the world but not interact with it.

I was not really sure why that happened. My skills focused with summoning the dead and binding them to the world. No one really delved deep into magic that summoned spirits and ghosts beyond the shamans and those were rare things in this day and age in this world.

On other worlds beyond the Alter-plane the barrier separating this dimension from the one that most magical beings left to roam there are plenty of shamans that could answer that question depending on the world.

"I understand that Alex is a wizard so what are you?" Ethan asked.

"He is a vampire." I answered.

"Seriously?" Ethan asked. "Shouldn't you be in Washington fighting a werewolf over Bella Swan?"

I watched as Marcus's eye began to twitch.

"Alex, can you bring this kid to a physical body for a bit?" Marcus asked cracking each of his fingers with his thumb.

"Why?" I asked.

"I want the satisfaction of killing this kid myself." Marcus said.

"How about we get along and focus on taking down the dark wizard we are already after." I said pointing to the fence and the field beyond.

"How do you plan to do that?" Marcus asked. "I can barely look at the place."

"I can take care of that. Just watch." I said as I reached into my coat and pulled out a laser pointer.

"What am I supposed to be looking at?" Marcus asked.

"One of my enchanted items. I am still working on a name to call it. I am stuck between Silver Stealer or Crimson Ray." I said pointing it at the field.

"What are you going to do with that?" Marcus asked.

I pressed the button to show him. Normal laser pointers just pointed a small beam of red light useful for annoying people and tricking cats. My laser pointer absorbed the prana from completed spells.

Which meant the warehouse was no longer hidden and the effect covering the field was gone as well.

"Whoa." Ethan said.

Given the proper respect by the pale teenager I put my laser pointer back in my jacket and pulled out my wand from the same pocket.

"Yes, I am awesome. Always remember that." I said as I gripped the fence and jumped over. "Come on."

I walked up to the side entrance of the warehouse where trucks would pick up and drop off packages and pointed my palm on the steel gate.

"Are you planning to blow the gate open?" Ethan asked me.

"Yes, Yes I am." I told him as I placed my hand on the door to aim on where the spell should hit to cause the most damage yet not send shrapnel to hurt me.

It was mostly my concern as I was the only one of the three of us present that could be hurt with an injury that would not heal.

"Why?" He asked me.

"Because I want to." I told him as I pulled my hand back.

In my mind it was a perfect reason to give. However, it seemed that it wasn't efficient enough to convince Ethan.

"Do you think that he has abandoned this location?" Ethan asked. "Think about it for a moment. What if he has cameras inside that warn him that someone has entered? That someone with magic is chasing him."

"Yes, that is true he would be more on guard if I destroyed the door." I acknowledged Ethan statement for what would happen if I showed no restraint.

"Don't listen to him. Blow the door up." Marcus cheered me on.

I took a deep breath before I aimed my wand at the chosen spot.

"Vehementi impetu." I chanted and sent a wave of force to open things rather violently.

The warehouse side door was blasted inward and bent in half and was blasted all the way to the back wall.

"Seriously?" Ethan asked as he gripped his head with both hands. "Are you insane? Why would you do that? I thought that we agreed it would be bad if the killer learned someone was here."

"Only a cowardly thief sneaks out in the night. When you slam through with your head held high and a song in your heart you are a true champion." I boasted paraphrasing what I heard a brave Macedonian king once say.

Ethan just slapped his face with both of his hands clearly annoyed with me.

"Seriously though the reason that I did this to panic and look over his shoulder. When faced with an unexpected surprises people tended to fall into familiar habits. They tended to go to places that made them feel safe. Having him hide in a location that he believed was safe would make it easier to track and find him. It would also make it rather hard for the killer to make any more victims." I said looking at him with a smile.

I would not deny that a part of me enjoyed breaking through the door as well. "Anyway, now let us go and see what is on the inside."

"Before I go in there do you think that the killer has any security measures in there?" Marcus asked.

"I doubt it." I answered while looking at the entrance. "Anyway, when we go inside, we should split up. We are looking for anything that might give us a clue to what the killer is planning."

I believed that these murders were part of a ritual if I was right about the symbols that had been placed on Ethan's body. Sacrificial magic to be specific but what I didn't get was why he was targeting non-magical people. In sacrificial magic the sacrifices were important both symbolically and magically. The more power the offering had the stronger the practitioner got so why would the killer target Ethan who was a regular person with not an ounce of magical talent.

"I still believe that blasting the door in was completely unnecessary." Ethan said as he followed behind me. "Isn't magic for the good of other people and to protect the innocent?"

With that question, I assumed that he had watched a lot of Charmed when he was alive.

Personally, I wasn't that big a fan of the show given the main characters had to be so selfless. To the point that they could not even enjoy the magic that they had been given.

"Not really. I was taught that helping people is important and if you can help you should make the effort, but I also learned that there are limits. Times when you should be selfish and look out for yourself." I told him. "Breaking in here made me feel better."

I looked through the hall. Motivational posters barely clung to the wall. I trailed my finger on the wall and learned that dust hung to the boards tighter than tape.

This place would be a nightmare for those with asthma.

"What kind of person taught you that?" Ethan asked.

"My teacher." I told him glancing into an office. "Growing a sense of self- preservation was important. If I volunteered for every reckless experiment or idea, he had then I doubt I would have made it to my current age."

I would have said high school graduation but I did not want to taunt Ethan with what he would never have.

"What kind of crazy teacher did you have?" Ethan asked.

"I don't want to talk about it." I answered feeling a shiver run down my spine at the memories of my education while walking into the office.

"What is he doing now because if that how you react then I fear for the world?" Ethan asked me.

"He's gone." I answered while opening a drawer looking for papers or other items.

All I found were paper clips and pens. They mocked me with their uselessness.

"How did he die?" Ethan asked solemnly.

"What made you think he died?" I asked, raising my head from the desk, and turning to him with wide eyes. "Man, I know you teenagers are angst ridden and dark but not every time a person says someone is gone does that mean they died."

Ethan looked like he was about to yell at me again before he took a deep breath. "What do you think that you will find in there?"

I moved to another desk cubicle and pulled out the chair.

"I am wondering when the last time this office was in use." I answered looking down in the drawer. "Found something."

The item that I had found was a calendar with the days marked off and there was a date marked with a red circle.

"So, this warehouse has been abandoned for two years." Ethan said looking at the calendar.

I feared what had happened to the people that had been working here. Still, I could not focus on that.

"Let's continue looking." I said, pulling back from the chair and standing up.

"Where is your teacher then?" Ethan asked.

"Oh, he is on another planet ruling as god-king." I said and could tell that he was shocked at what I said.

I walked through a door that led to the storage and loading area.

The shelves were empty and covered in dust, there were broken shards of glass that used to be windows, and there were broken pieces of wood that had been intended to be furniture lying about.

"What do you mean he is ruling a kingdom on another planet?" Ethan asked when he stopped being stunned and caught up with me.

"Death is terrifying. Even for those with magic." I said and looked down on a large circle that looked to be drawn in chalk surrounded with sigils. "Well wizard and witches have decided to fight that fear by becoming immortal. My teacher is just one of the few that have managed to achieve that desire."

I started moving around the circle taking pictures of the sigils with my phone so I could check my books and see if anything matched. I doubted it but just in case I wanted to have images to reference later.

"Okay I am with you so far but how does that end up with your teacher becoming a god?" Ethan asked me.

"Well, my teacher gained immortality but like all people he wanted something more." I told him while texting Marcus that we had found something. "He wanted to use that power to gain more. So, my teacher found out the way to achieve power on the level of a demigod. From there he worked his way to create his own planet to rule over as god-king."

I kept the story short as he did not need the long explanation and I did not want to look back upon traumatic memories of the deadly missions he had sent me on to get the ingredients.

"How did he do it?" Ethan asked.

"I have no idea." I answered with a scowl. "Public wizard/witch tradition is that you either figured it out on your own or you should accept your failure and just die a lot later than non-magical people."

"Your people are just fine with that?" Ethan asked.

"It is the way with teacher's and apprentices." I said returning to my original position.

They had the answers, but they rarely told their students wanting to see if they could figure it out on their own.

"Why did he leave?" Ethan asked.

"There is a treaty created by the magic council long ago for the protection of this planet." I answered.

Basically, it stated that as long as you won't cause a war on this planet and leave after you become immortal the council will grant you vast immunities with whatever you plan to do next or have done. For the Council it was not worth angering overpowered people in a fight that could destroy the planet just because you didn't like them. Before that treaty though they were fair game.

Lots of thrill seekers wanted to take the challenge and gain the title of god-hunter.

"Aren't you afraid that they are going to eventually launch a war against each other?" Ethan asked.

"There are so many worlds and so few immortals that they do not believe that will be a concern for a very long time." I told Ethan and we both turned around when we heard the sound of feet clanging and met the sight of Marcus running down the steps from above.

"What are you running from?" I asked him concerned.

Part of the concern was for him but mostly it was for me. I doubted that it had been a spider that had sent him running.

"You will see them soon enough!" He shouted, pointing at the path he came from.

I blinked a couple times to make sure I wasn't seeing things. Chasing after Marcus were seven suits of armor all with glowing red eyes and big sharp swords. They were colored a dark silver, their glowing eyes looked hungry for blood, and it felt like they wouldn't be happy until they got it.

I guess I was wrong. The killer did have guards here.

"I thought you said there were no security measures?" Ethan questioned me with scared eyes.

It seemed that with his panic he had forgotten that he wasn't flesh and blood anymore and couldn't be killed.

"I assumed so." I said as I observed the coming threat. "Who puts guards inside an invisible building?"

"Why didn't you destroy them?" Ethan asked Marcus. "Don't vampires have supernatural strength?"

"I wasn't risking getting myself cut up by those swords I figured why not let the wizard deal with it." Marcus said.

I used their seconds of conversation to think of a plan.

"Both of you shut up." I said conjuring a sword for Marcus to use to defend himself. "Here is where we will make our stand."

"Really a sword?" Marcus complained. "Why don't you just conjure up a rocket launcher and end this mess?"

He was only doing so to be a pain. If he wanted to, he could run, and these things would never catch up with him.

"Complain less and fight more." I told him bringing out my pen from the inside chest pocket of my jacket.

"A pen?" Ethan questioned. "What good is that going to be in this situation?"

He still hadn't learnt one of the most important rules of knowing magic.

Never doubt the wizard.

I did not hold it against him. We had not even known each other for a full day yet. He would learn soon enough though.

I twirled my blue pen in my hand and uncapped it with my mind and forcing the point at them he saw my pen change into a sword. It was the length of my hand with the guard a dull bronze and the handle was brown. The blade was silver with writing on it that glowed blue. It was in my opinion a thing of beauty and destruction. When swung it would glow blue.

"Why is your pen a sword?" Ethan asked.

Truthfully because people were less likely to pay attention to a man running with a pen in his hand compared to a person running with a weapon in his hand.

I was not going to say that though.

"People say the pen is mightier than the sword, but I wanted to rewrite that equation." I answered as I gripped the sword with both hands.

The pen was called the Infinite Armory. It could turn into any weapon. Sword, bow, halberd, lance, spear, and more. I just really liked it as a sword. In many fantasy stories I read the hero had a glowing sword in hand as he charged at unfortunate odds. His only defense being his sword and his willpower.

I did not have the plot armor of a fantasy hero, but I would have a magic sword.

"He has practiced that line for a while" Marcus whispered to Ethan "Probably hoping that whoever heard it thought that it was cool. I think it is because he wanted to be able to swing a lightsaber at people."

He just had to go and ruin my one-liner.

CHAPTER 11

So, there we were a vampire, a wizard, and a spirit being charged at by suits of armor. I am pretty sure this could be the start of a joke.

"I blame you for this." Ethan said scowling.

"Hey, we are trying to solve your murder." I said as I looked at the seven suits of armor moving towards us.

"How do you want to handle this?" Marcus asked as he gripped his sword and faced forward.

"I had been thinking that you take the six on the left and I'll take the one on the right." I told him ready to charge and fight the knights.

"That better be a joke because if it's not I'm leaving now." Marcus warned.

"Of course, I'm joking." I told him with a smile that I thought was reassuring but I do not think he believed me given the glare he gave me.

"Is there anything that I can do to help?" Ethan asked.

That was a horrible idea. Each instance that Ethan got hurt would require my magic to reform him and that was not something I needed during this fight.

"No." I said. "I want you to stay up on those steps and keep an eye out in case we get distracted."

We knew nothing about sword fighting but I was hopeful it was the same for them given that they couldn't think and probably never learned. That they would stick with certain patterns like NPCs in videogames. The downside of that argument was that since they weren't flesh and bone, they would not get tired. They were animated by magic so they could go on for as long as the magic kept powering them.

I had a limit on how much magic I could use and even Marcus could be taken down easily if he was overwhelmed.

As my current situation proved.

"Let's get our Jedi on." I cried out as we charged the armor.

I could hear the clanging of steel that came from Marcus and his four targets. Any other time I would have been excited to see knights fight a vampire but now was not the time. I ran forward heading towards the three remaining knights.

My eyes were focused as I charged at the suit in front and felt my hands ring when the swords met.

His swing was heavier than I expected. I would have to end this quickly because swords fighting was exhausting, and I wasn't a fan of actual exercise. Casting magic took a lot of energy and so I had never needed to do heavy exercise since I started learning. I really regretted that at the moment as I had to move between the empty knights and pay attention to three different swords.

I now know how they felt during the second movie when they had to fight the droid army.

The Jedi had it easy their swords were made of light and could cut through steel like it was butter. My sword may look magical, but it was originally just a pen that was enchanted to turn into any weapon I desired I could tell that my sword was close to breaking, and I was not surprised. The point of this weapon was variability not durability.

My enchantment on the pen gave it what I thought was the appearance and durability of the weapon I was using but given that I had done no research on how swords were made they were at best just estimates.

I could feel the sword getting heavier in my hands and I felt like dropping it, but I knew the moment I did would be the minute I would be losing my head.

Obviously, I liked my head so I couldn't let that happen. So, I just gritted my teeth and moved to parry another downwards sword strike.

Hearing a cracking sound, I looked down and saw the sword that I was using was no longer glowing and it had cracks running all over it. I hoped that it would not break but the universe did not grant my wish. The sword shattered and broke into pieces.

It was so broken that it didn't even turn back into a pen.

I would have to make a new one when I had the time. I held the broken bronze guard of the sword and looked at a sword swing through the air and was about to make contact with my head. I closed my eyes and prepared to do something I thought was totally reckless.

I teleported to the other side of the warehouse.

Most people would wonder if you could teleport why didn't you do so when you were fighting?

The reason for that was pretty simple. I only used teleportation when I was in a calm state of mind. I wasn't fond of accidents happening if I made a mistake when I teleported. I had read in books and seen many movies about what happens if you aren't focused on teleporting or if you are thinking of something else.

It was another reason I drove a car.

Looking over my shoulder I could see that Marcus was having a much better time than me. The sword I had made for him had broken a while ago but that didn't stop him. Marcus had ripped off the arm of one of the suits and stole its sword.

"Take this you tin bucket!" Ethan shouted, throwing broken furniture pieces at the suits to gain their attention.

I clenched my fingers and glared at the sensation. My arms felt like they were going to fall off and try to crawl away to escape this battle. I could not fight with a sword anymore. Even raising my wand and keeping it focused would be a struggle.

That did not mean that I could not use magic. However, without a wand I would spend more energy than I wanted. In that case There was truly only one way that I was going to hit any of them as exhausted as I was. That was by overwhelming firepower.

So much so that they couldn't even resist.

"Ignis-pila Rapidus." I said and watched as forty fireballs the size of basketballs appeared over my head and swarmed at the living armor.

They may have been gifted the ability to move and fight but I doubt they would be able to survive being melted. Unfortunately, that didn't do anything besides making them heat up and become even harder to touch according to Marcus.

"Got any more brilliant ideas professor?" Marcus asked sarcastically.

There was clear irritation in his voice as he moved to dodge being the flames.

Vampires were extremely flammable. If they caught on fire, they would have to smother the flame out or it would spread all over their bodies until they burned to death. There were other ways to kill vampires, but fire was one of the easiest ways.

So, it was no surprise that he wasn't happy even though he was in no danger of being burned.

"Not finished yet!" I shouted back at him trying to hide the fact that I was making this up as I went along and that I didn't accidentally almost roast him like a chicken.

"Sonum aquarum." I cast and flowing from my hands were jets of water that blasted the suits of armor whole.

"Now are you finished?" Marcus asked throwing a sword through the chest piece of the fake knight.

"The more you ask the longer it takes." I told Marcus hoping he would shut up and let me focus.

He unfortunately didn't take the advice and had to say something.

"Move quicker then and I won't ask." Marcus snarked.

I decided to ignore him and focus back on what I was doing. I would have to work on my wandless casting later because I was taking too long and the only reason, I made it this long is because Marcus was fighting most of them.

"Frigidus Ventus." I said a cold wind began to blow over the warehouse and the suits still tried to walk forwards.

I had intended to freeze them however we watched as they eventually began to slow down, and I could tell that it was becoming harder and harder for them to move.

"Looks like they had more iron than their silver coating suggested." I said.

"What did you to them?" Ethan asked as we watched them oxidize.

"I made them rust." I explained.

Just like the tinman from wizard of Oz they may have been able to move and fight without loss of stamina, but they were still made of metal. When metal was exposed to both water and wind the result was obvious.

"Not a bad plan for something you made up on the spot." Marcus said picking up the arm of the knight suit that he had chopped off earlier.

"You assume that it wasn't my plan from the beginning." I told Marcus.

"Then that was a terrible plan." Marcus said as he leaned on the stolen sword. "You look like you are about to fall. It would have been easier if you just used that laser pointer of yours. We wouldn't have needed to have that ridiculous sword fight at all."

Having lost that conversation just closed my mouth and began looking around the room. There were burn marks where the fire had been spreading before they were extinguished by my water spell. This place was a mess before we got here but now it was even worse after we were through with it.

However even after all of that the question remained. What were we going to do with this place?

I could burn down the building and see if that made me feel better about this entire mess, but I think that would be an overreaction. I could have Marcus hypnotize people near here into remembering this place but what would be the point? It had disappeared from the records of whichever company owned this place long ago.

I walked outside the entrance I had made when I broke down the door and took a good look at the building.

"Marcus I have a plan for the building. Tell Ethan. You two should really hurry up out of there." I said with a grin knowing that he could hear me.

I felt a moment of inspiration and I wanted to see that dream become reality. I had figured out what I was going to do to the building that no one remembered, and I really didn't want anybody on the inside of it when I was working.

As Marcus and Ethan walked out of the building I grinned and grabbed my wand. After everything that had happened it was easy to push past the pain as I pointed it at the warehouse.

"What are you planning to do?" Ethan asked concerned with the grin on my face.

"Don't worry about it." I said and he turned away, just shaking his head.

"Facere Parvum." I said chanting the words four times and the building shrunk down to keychain size.

"That's it?" Marcus asked looking at the space that used to belong to the warehouse. "You just made it small I thought you were going to do something completely exciting."

"Now he will definitely notice that someone with magic is after him." Ethan said.

"If he learns that his warehouse has been stolen it might move his plans back months." I said, turning to them. "Maybe he will even slip up making it that much easier for us to catch him."

"You are risking a lot of people's lives." Ethan said before walking away from us.

"It's part of a bigger plan." I said, throwing the warehouse up and down in my hand and walking to the car.

"Where are we headed next?" Marcus asked.

"Now we are going after the next location on the list." I answered as I put the warehouse on the dashboard of my car.

"Are you sure that we should continue?" Ethan asked. "This case is turning way harder than I was told at the beginning. Maybe we should just ask the council to look into this."

"You two should try to be more optimistic." I said as I shifted the wheel and started driving away. "I believe that this team can take down this killer.

I had been arrested by the police and almost killed by suits of armor. I did not want to hand it off to anyone else. I wanted to learn who the killer was, how he had killed Ethan, and why he was going through all of this effort.

I cannot say that I did not get my wish.

CHAPTER 12

I stood outside my car and looked at Wissinoming park. It was the next closest spot on the map that I had found traces of the dark magic that the killer had used. On my way here I had worried that this was the next site I was going to discover a grave similar to the one given to Ethan in Northwood Park.

As I looked around all I could wonder was what this killer had against parks.

"Ethan this is where you come in." I commanded him. "I want you to phase through the ground and see if there is anything there."

After my last attempt I was not fond of the idea of digging up another corpse buried in a park. After all the last time I had been in such a situation had not ended so well for me. I would have preferred to not have to see another police precinct for a long time.

However, this time would be different as I didn't have to do any digging at all.

"What?" Ethan asked.

"How would I even do that?"

"You are a spirit now. That means you have the capability to turn invisible, intangible, and can fly." I explained. "The old rules do not apply to you now. Just imagine that you want to phase through the ground, and you will."

Before Ethan had died and been summoned back to the world of the living, he had been a regular person. A lot of entertainment liked to use that a flesh and blood body came with limitations. Bound by the laws of physics and the forces of nature. That to protect their body from overtaxing itself evolution had created certain blocks in the mind and body of humanity.

"Why do I have to do it?" He questioned me like he could change my mind if he argued enough. "Can't you use magic to move the dirt?"

I tried the same thing when I was his age and just like when I tried it, he would fail too.

"I am still recovering from the fight with the suits of armor. Plus, you're the spirit and can phase through the ground without getting exhausted or covered in dirt." I told him.

"I think it's because I'm the youngest and you're just lazy." He complained.

While that may be true, I was not going to tell him that.

"You want to help me solve this mystery or not?" I asked and waved him onward.

Ethan spent a few minutes grumbling my decision before he walked into the park and sunk under the ground.

I walked into the park to look around. Making sure there was no trap waiting to be sprung here while I waited for Casper the brooding ghost to return.

A branch snapped behind me. I turned and was prepared to blast whatever was trying to sneak up on me when I saw that it was Marcus. Gripping my chest until I calmed back down until my heart was back to its normal rhythm.

I glared at him and the broken pieces of the stick that he was holding in his hands.

"Glad to see that I have your attention." Marcus said as he dropped the sticks.

"I want to talk to you. Can Ethan hear us right now?"

"No. If there are bodies buried underground, they are probably rather deep." I answered.

"I was wondering if you had talked to Ethan about his aunt being missing?" Marcus asked.

"Not yet." I answered him as I raised my head to look at him.

"When do you plan to tell him?" Marcus asked. "After the case is over and before you send him back to where you summoned him from?"

"It would be better for him to leave with answers than work with worries." I said.

A depressed spirit would just bring angst to the group.

"You are assuming that his aunt's disappearance has anything to do with this case." Marcus said. "If it doesn't, he is going to spend the rest of his afterlife wondering. what happened to her."

"Why do you care so much?" I asked. "This case was just supposed to be a passing interest to you."

"I respect the honor and power of family." Marcus said. "Having a relative just vanish into nothing is not a curse I would ever place on someone."

I wondered if his feeling were due to his transformation into a vampire. Perhaps he left his family with questions after it happened?

I heard a snap and found Marcus standing in front of me.

"You need to stop living in your dream world and pay attention." Marcus said.

"I want to figure a way to say it without hurting the kid." I said.

"Alright." Marcus said with a reluctant nod as he stepped back.

I should have known that it would not end so easily. That he would force my hand. Ten minutes after our conversation Ethan rose from the earth with a frown on his face.

"Did you see any bodies down there?" I asked him.

"Yeah, there are bodies buried under there." He said angrily as he looked at the ground.

"How many?" I asked while fearing the answer.

"I saw at least four." Ethan answered. "They are about twenty feet below the ground."

"What?" I asked, horrified at the number of people that were buried under this park.

I had assumed that the dark wizard would intend to make more victims for whatever scheme he had up and running but I had not wanted to assume that he already had so many. Given that there were other sites that I had yet to search in I feared that we would be met with more of the same.

"Do you think that there are bodies buried under the warehouse?" Ethan asked.

"I cannot say for certain. We can find that out after we catch the person behind this." I said.

When I had been searching for traces, I had limited my range to the city. There could be more places where he dumped the bodies. Maybe across state lines? Maybe even across the east coast?

"Why do you think he is killing all these people?" Marcus asked.

That question broke me from my worries.

"I believe this number of sacrifices means that he was very weak and wanted to get stronger." I said. "Now I am just hoping that the killer only had enough magic to lift a pencil and that charging his weapon took decades of work. I also hope that after all of these murders that he only has the same amount of power that a regular spell caster would have normally."

I still have that hope.

The other opinion that I theorized but did not want to say is that he already had enough power but was working his way up to do something tremendous. Something that would be beyond belief for a single caster.

Still either way I would hope for the best and prepare for a mountain of doom to rise in the city.

"The universe truly does enjoy making you suffer." Marcus said. "You should get a mug made at the end of this job."

"All I am hoping for is to live to see to see the end of the job." I said.

"So, who is going to do the digging?" Ethan asked as raised his head to look at us.

"Him." Marcus and I pointed at each other simultaneously.

"I'm not doing it." I told him and I was determined to win the conversation.

"Well, I'm not doing it." Marcus said as he looked at his nails.

"Are you worried about you nails?" I asked. "They'll grow back. Plus, you will be using a shovel."

I was irritated. He wanted me to have a difficult conversation with Ethan but he refused to dig a simple hole.

"I joined this case to help you solve Ethan's murder." Marcus said as he raised his head to look at me. "Not to dig holes in the ground. I did enough of that during my summer jobs when I was alive to learn that I hated it."

"Then what are we going to do?" I questioned him. "We can't just abandon them here now that we know."

I watched as Marcus thought for a few seconds before getting a grin.

"It is at a time like this that I am glad I am so careful." Marcus said as he pulled out his cellphone and dialed a number. "Captain Bennet this is Marcus. We are at Wissonming park and need the assistance of a few officers from your precinct. We believe that we have found a set of bodies and need help excavating them."

He then hung up and snapped the phone shut.

"Not a bad plan." I said with understanding.

It seems that his idea of hypnotizing the police to work with us could pay off even more than I had originally thought.

CHAPTER 13

For all his faults and there are many you could not say that Marcus was not a problem solver. With his control over Captain Bennet, it did not take long for a team to be sent to do the digging for us.

Ethan had been put back in the necklace because otherwise there would be questions asked that I was not going to answer.

I saw the detectives from earlier walking over in our direction and I will admit to not paying much attention to Detective O'Connell walking my way as I was focused entirely on Detective Langdon. Now that she wasn't trying to arrest me, I could see how pretty she was.

I had always liked women with green eyes and red hair. In the words of Carl Carlton, she was a Bad Mama Jama.

A wind began to blow and while I consider all winds at night to be ominous, I wasn't paying much attention to that all I could see was Detective Langdon. Everything else had disappeared, there was only me and her.

There she was standing on a walkway and walking down like a model. How it got there I had no idea, but I wasn't really in the mood to solve that mystery I was fine right where I was wearing a red jacket and tight pants and as she got closer, she was taking pulling off her jacket revealing a white shirt that she was unbuttoning however just as I was getting to the good part I was brought back to reality.

A shake to the shoulder drew me from my daydream.

I turned towards the person who I was sure that I was going to be hexing and saw Marcus grinning at me. I glared at him even harder. Vampires could not hypnotize anything else that was supernatural, but they could read their minds and influence their thoughts on others with illusions if they got a hand on them.

"Don't put weird ideas in my head." I told him backing up out of his grasp.

"That was all you buddy, I was just making sure that you remembered where we were." He said with a smirk.

I glared at him until he took five steps back from me.

"You know if you can spend this much time glaring at me you can take that time and ask her out." Marcus said.

"This is neither the right time or place." I said as I gestured around the park and the dead bodies that the police were here to dig up.

Marcus just shook his head.

"If you concern yourself with every place crime or violence has happened then you aren't going to ask anyone out." Marcus said.

Then he turned to the detectives and walked over to them.

A few seconds passed before I realized how bad an idea that would be and moved to follow after them.

Marcus was always trying to get me out of my comfort zone and be more outgoing. My belief is that his confidence came from his immortality. You could be as shameless as you wanted when everyone around you was going to lose their memories with time.

Unlike him I didn't have that security blanket.

I wasn't the outgoing type. The thing is I preferred to not interact with other people beyond what was needed. Hanging out with groups was fine. I wouldn't have to do any serious talking. All that was required was me throwing in a joke here or there. A nod to show that I was paying attention. That was something I was good at.

I was introverted and I liked it that way.

People always wanted to talk about feelings and do things. I was more into reading books and learning magic than partying in clubs. I should care more but that struggle was something I had my entire life to work on.

The plan was to rush right at them and stop Marcus from whatever he was scheming but I got there too late and only heard the end of their conversation.

"… So, you can see my friend is too shy to ask you out, so I am going to do it for him, and you are going to say yes." Marcus said and as I pulled him back, I saw his eyes turn back to their natural brown.

"Okay here." She said and took out a piece of paper to write her number and then she gave it to me.

"What in the world did you do that for?" I asked him as I grabbed his arm.

"Oh, don't complain I knew it would take you forever to ask her out, so I did it for you." Marcus said as he broke free of my grip.

It was not a surprise that Marcus did not get my issue with his attempt.

Marcus is a distrustful person by nature. He claimed that he used his hypnotism to keep people around him "honest". He believed that people had made a mess of the world with free will by making stupid decisions. Mistakes that are created by a corrupt ambition fueled by selfish greed.

So, he only respected the idea of other people's free will to a certain point. He let them believe that they could tell him their opinion and beliefs but if he felt that it was stupid, he would change the person's mind so quickly that their hats would still be falling to the ground when he was finished.

In my opinion it was a matter of control. As long as everything in his area worked out in a manner that he could understand then he could remain in his content lifestyle.

Some would argue that I was a hypocrite. That I used his abilities when it was convenient and complained when it was inconvenient. Let people say what they want. My job involved lying to people so what is a little sprinkle of hypocrisy added to the top of the ice cream cone. Some would argue that we did not have the right to change the opinions of people at a whim. I would argue that some ideas could be dangerous and were rather hard to eliminate so hypnotizing them away created less victims when the stubborn and hateful refused to bend.

That did not mean that there were not lines drawn in the sand.

"Still now I will never know if it was because you hypnotized her, or she truly liked me." I told him and glared at him.

"So, what do you want me to do about it?" He asked me while giving a sigh.

He couldn't use his powers on me so I wouldn't forget, and I would not give up on this, so he knew the only option was to give in to my demands to shut me up.

"Fix it. I can deal with you having them help us but that is it." I told him as I held the piece of paper in my hand in front of him and crumpled it up.

I would not be made to feel guilty.

It didn't take more than three minutes for Marcus to fix everything he did and send her on her way remembering not a bit of her previous conversation with Marcus and me since he called her here.

"Alex, you really need to relax and not over think things." Marcus told me.

"I really wish that I could do just that, but it was not the way that I work." I told him.

"You just need to change your way of thinking." Marcus told me.

Like it was such a simple decision.

"I don't like change and I do not need any help." I told him but was certain that he wouldn't listen.

This was another one of his faults. Besides being impulsive he was also very stubborn.

"You need to focus on winning." He told me with a grin on his face.

"Winning?" I questioned him wondering what he meant.

I felt like he was referencing something, but it was still escaping me.

"Yeah. You are a wizard just make a potion to increase your luck and aggression. I will get you the tiger blood and all the other ingredients you will need. Just focus on making it perfect." He told me.

I could see he was counting up the things he imagined would fit in this potion.

"Isn't that what drove Charlie Sheen crazy?" I asked him as I realized the reference he was making.

"He's still doing movies and television shows, so I say he is doing all right with the amount he has." Marcus said.

We would have kept talking except Detective O'Connell decided to leave the officer digging up the bodies and move to interrupt us.

"Spencer, Gus if you have had any visions of where to go to next it would be appreciated?" He mocked us.

He may not have remembered us from our time in the precinct but by going by the look on his face he still didn't like us.

"I am deeply insulted by that remark detective." Marcus answered back. I could tell he wasn't going to let this go and prepared myself.

"Oh really?" Detective O'Connell said with scorn and contained anger. "I am so sorry for insulting people wasting the time and resources of actual detectives. If I could arrest the both of you for obstructing justice I would."

"Yes. I see myself more like a more fashionable James Carter and Alex is my discount Detective Lee." Marcus said.

"Really?" I questioned him the anger clear in my voice. "I think you both are being pretty insulting right now."

"What you are too light to be Carter and you aren't Asian, so I had to make some substitutions for the reference to work." Marcus said looking too pleased with himself. "Or I would have called us Agent M and Agent A of Division Six."

I was going to make sure to remember this. A consequence of not being able to let things go led me to being a very petty person when I wanted to be. All I had to wait for was the right moment.

"I am the reference guy and both of you are trying to steal my shtick." I said glaring at Marcus.

"You are the psychic detective. The Straight man." Marcus argued. "You can't also be the guy that does the comedy act. The bit doesn't work then. Have you never seen a buddy cop movie?"

"The problem is that people don't laugh at your jokes." I said.

"Alright I find the both of you annoying." Detective O'Connell said. "Why don't you two get some distance and figure this out. Let the police do the work and the real detectives find out who is behind all this."

"Harsh but fair Detective O'Connell. Harsh but fair." I said nodding as I moved to cover Marcus's mouth before he could say anything else.

He started to struggle and break free.

"Time to move on." I said.

He reluctantly allowed himself to be pulled away to the car.

I was happy to get out of there. That park was full of bad juju as some would say. I was sure that unless an exorcism was performed on the area that a whole bunch of nastiness would find itself attracted to it.

"There's no way I am letting him get the last word like that." Marcus said as he pulled out his phone and started to type a text message.

"Marcus come on we aren't needed there." I told him and he glared at me.

"That is one of your main problems. You need more confidence man; you have magic you shouldn't be afraid to confront others." Marcus said turning to look at the bulldozer that was driving onto the field to dig up the bodies.

"You seriously don't get it." I told him while looking at the shrunken warehouse.

"Explain it to me then." He demanded.

"Remember we called the police to get the corpses out of the park." I told him as I placed the necklace in the back seat let Ethan out. "Waiting here and arguing with Detective O'Connell was just a waste of time when we have other locations to look into."

I could see his eyes lighting up as he realized what was going on.

"Ah-ha. Solve the case before the detective and then rub his nose in it?" He questioned.

"After the police finish digging up the bodies, they are going to be too busy investigating who they were, so we should have plenty of time to figure this out ourselves." I said.

"Can we move past the petty desire to show up a hardworking detective." Ethan asked as he moved forward in the car. "What are you going to tell the police when we catch the guy?"

"What do you mean?" I asked.

"I don't think that the police are going to give up on hunting this guy now that they have found his other victims. Serial killers tend to make the news." Ethan said. "How do you plan to make all of this go away?"

"He does raise an interesting point." Marcus said. "Supernatural dramas and Sci-fi shows always have a pair of investigators looking into cases that ended in mysterious ways and unexplained deaths."

"I doubt that the detectives plan to just close the folder, put them away in some locker, and moved on to next week's problem." Ethan said.

I did not intend to let that happen at the end of this case. I did not want to rely on the thread of hope that no one became interested in such events and this file never saw the light of day again.

"I am going to look into way to solve that problem." I told him. "I don't know how yet but I am going to solve this case in a way that both the police and I could have a happy ending."

I deserved a hard slap to the back of my head for my arrogance.

CHAPTER 14

"Where are we driving to?" Ethan asked as he turned to face me.

"The next spot on the map. It felt like it had the deepest residue of the killer's mana. I believe that it could be his house." I said grimly.

This was the strongest source so I had wanted to avoid it until we couldn't anymore but with at least a handful of people dead I did not want to wait a moment longer.

"That's great news." Ethan said as he slammed his fist into his hand. "We surprise him, and we can put an end to all of this."

He was so optimistic I did not feel like crushing his hopes with doubt.

Ten minutes later we drove up the street and we finally saw the house. All in all, it looked like a regular house. It was a single building that looked to have three floors given by the windows. It was made of brown bricks, and it had a roof that was painted white that had tiles that looked like they were beginning to fall off. There was an iron fence and a driveway that was missing a car.

If my sense of caution had sound, then back then it was ringing like a fire truck siren.

I had seen too many movies and read too many books to not be suspicious of normal-looking houses. Even more so when I knew they belonged to dangerous criminals.

"I was not expecting this." Marcus said looking to the left and out his window.

"What do you mean?" I asked as I looked around. "Were you expecting it to be a creaky rundown building under a singular dark cloud with rain and lightning falling around it?"

"I expected something creepier for a house that belonged to an evil wizard." Ethan said.

"Exactly." Marcus agreed as he snapped his fingers.

"If you ever read any book from Stephen King that involved Maine, you would be suspicious of a house like this." I said. "The houses and cities that looked like nothing bad could ever happen were the places where the craziest things were found."

That was one of the reasons I planned to never visit that state.

"Is this about your list?" Marcus asked.

"His list?" Ethan asked.

"He has an entire list with the names of places that he is never going to visit." Marcus said. "Some places scare him so much that he has the locations underlined in red ink six times."

"Make fun of my list." I said as I drove to the end of the street. "When you have looked into the eyes of seven Senikla spiders you can say my fears are ridiculous."

"Senikla spiders?" Ethan asked.

"Spiders the size of pandas with fangs the length of knives with hallucinogenic venom." I answered shivering as I turned the car and drove behind the house.

We did not need to be seen breaking into a house in broad daylight.

"Do you hear anything?" I asked Marcus.

"No." Marcus denied with a shake of his head. "It seems that whoever was living here wasn't home at the moment."

"We missed him." Ethan said as he slammed his hand on the door.

Then I started thinking that perhaps it was not optimism moving him forwards. "Are we still going to try and get inside?" Marcus asked.

"We need to learn who he is." I said.

"This is the reason that white people die in horror movies." Marcus said.

"Don't worry. When we split up, I have no intention of going to the attic or the basement." I said with a smile. "Not to mention that you are going to be walking in front of me."

"You say that you are a believer in free will, but you use me as a sacrificial pawn." Marcus complained.

"I am not forcing you." I said. "Though I will remind you that we are hunting a dark wizard that is killing innocent people."

"You are lucky that I care about the lives of innocent people." Marcus said as he opened his door.

I followed him out of the car and faced the house. There was a tree in the yard covering the grass and the backdoor in its shadow.

"Just be ready if a trap activates like in the warehouse." Marcus said as he walked forward.

I nodded and pulled my wand out of my coat pocket on the right side and was prepared for anything.

"How do you fit all that stuff in there?" Ethan asked.

Everything seemed fine for now, so I decided to show him.

I pulled pens from my pockets and switched where I put them and where I pulled them from. We ignored the sounds around us of someone fighting with a door and losing.

"How did you do that?" Ethan asked completely curious.

I tried hard to keep the grin off my face. I had created it just so someone would ask that very question.

"My coat's enchanted. The pockets are all interconnected, so I have everything I need when I need it." I explained to him. "It had taken me months to get the spell work on this thing right and in my opinion, it was one of my greatest enchantments."

This enchantment on the coat was based on the concept of hammer space. The ability that allows cartoon characters to pull large objects from pockets.

With just a thought I could stuff or pull-out items through my coat. I had the same enchantment on my five coats in case something happened to one and it couldn't be fixed for some reason. If in the event that the coat is stolen, then it was designed to turn into a normal coat and if it got in the hands of another witch or wizard then it would turn to dust.

Being a wizard meant you had to think a few steps ahead.

"I could use some help over here." Marcus said annoyed as he got up from the ground.

While I had been explaining to Ethan the greatness of my coat, he had been trying to get in for the last five minutes and nothing he was doing was having an effect.

It was as I looked back on moment like that, I found humor in my darkening situation.

Marcus first tried opening the door and when that didn't help, he began trying to break down the door with brute force. After his third punch the door began to bounce him back more painfully with each following attempt.

Looking at him I could see that the suit that he was wearing was covered in dirt and the sleeves were ripped. I wondered how hard his falls were and then I remembered his interference with the detective and felt a sense of satisfaction that he was getting beaten up by a door.

"All right just calm down and wait for a bit." I told them and headed to the trunk to my car.

I had plenty of ways around a barrier that was created to keep unfriendly people out but for the quickest way I needed things that were in my car. Opening the trunk and the suitcase that was in it I grabbed a pen and a few slips of paper and brought them back to the others.

Art had not been one of my top skills when I was younger. Stick figures were prominent in my work. Even then my teacher thought that cavemen had more skill at art than I. However, as I started learning the different branches of magic, I figured why not use my style of art. I started learning pictomancy as it just needed belief in the image even if it could not be believed by anyone else.

That focus spread out as I figured out different applications for it.

These slips of paper were enchanted to both stick to whatever surface I chose and depending on the type of spell infused into it they had many purposes. I had based them off O-fuda. They were talismans that wizards and witches that originated or descended from the east liked to use.

The original use for O-fuda had been protection but I used them for a different purpose.

Times like this I was glad that I did not let him stop me. They didn't last long and were destroyed after one use, but we would not require that much time to walk through the door.

"What are slips of paper supposed to do?" Ethan asked.

It was strange that he was full of doubt even after seeing so much magic the past two days.

"Just watch." I said as I placed each slip of paper to the sides of the door and tapped them in clockwork order.

The images glowed blue before a portal opened that showed the inside of the house.

"Now we can pass." I told them and waved them through feeling smug that I got through the wards of the killer's house. "After you."

"You would be the nightmare of any bank or security system." Marcus said.

"Should we split up and search for clues?" Ethan asked after we had passed through the portal.

"You notice how it is the person that can sink through the ground that asks that question?" Marcus asked.

"What is that supposed to mean?" Ethan asked.

"Just that you have a way out in case you need to escape while we are trapped." Marcus said.

"Calm down." I said as I looked around. "If we were in a horror movie right now, we would be the in buildup so we should be safe for a while."

"Is that the same confidence that led to us fighting those suits of armor?" Marcus asked.

"Shut up and go look for clues. We need to learn about the killer that we are hunting." I said walking towards the stairs. "I will check the rooms upstairs. Marcus you can search the dining room, kitchen, and basement. Ethan, you look around this room and the backyard. If any of you need help scream quickly."

I reached the top of the stairs and took a look around. There were bedrooms at each end of the hall. Between the bedrooms looked to be a closet and a bathroom. I walked to the master bedroom. I was about to reach for the doorknob and turn it when I paused.

In the warehouse I had been overconfident because I believed that I passed through the trap that I had nothing to worry about. I had not expected the second defensive measure. If Marcus had not been a vampire, he could have died.

Pulling my hand back I pulled out a pair of sunglasses from my coat. These glasses were designed to let me see prana and mana. So, if there is a trap on the door, I would be able to see it.

There was nothing there. The door is clean. Now that I was sure that it was safe, I raised my glasses to my hair and opened the door.

When I stepped inside, I took a quick glance around the room. It was common enough and had all the regular things you would expect to find in an adult's room. A television on a dresser, a king-sized bed, a closet, opposing the bed was a Pittsburgh Steelers poster hanging on the wall, and there is a chest by the bed.

"What else can I learn about you?" I asked looking around. "I have just learned that you are not loyal to the state team."

There was something in this room that was bugging me, and I would not calm down until I figured it out.

I checked everything.

Inside the closet were extra clothes and sports jerseys from the Chicago Clubs baseball team. Inside the chest were books of poetry and cooking.

None of it was suspicious enough that it should be messing with me. My annoyance grew as each second passed. I took a deep breath to calm down and think. I had become aware of something without realizing it. In my experience that usually was the result of something magical. It could be the result of some enchantment in the room.

Luckily, I had the perfect tool for the job.

I pulled my glasses down and looked around the room for the enchanted item. Looking around the room I could see what had been bugging me. The entire room was covered in prana. It was especially thick on the wall behind the bed.

I texted Marcus to come upstairs and bring Ethan.

"I brought him." Marcus said as he looked around. "What happened?"

"Why are your hands wet?" I asked looking at Marcus who was wiping his hands on a paper towel.

"I had to wash them after I walked around the basement." Marcus said. "It is just like the warehouse in that a lot of the stuff down there needs a good dusting."

"You make fun of my fears and yet you ignore your fear of germs." I said.

"I do not have a fear of germs." Marcus denied.

"However, you are really uncomfortable with anything that wasn't clean." I said.

"A majority of people have that issue." Marcus said. "It's called being raised with standards."

"Did you find anything?" Ethan asked.

"I think so." I answered. "Did you guys find anything?"

"Look at this!" Ethan said holding up a brown wallet. "I have discovered the killer's identity. His name is Bryan Mercer."

"You found his wallet?" I asked as I walked to Ethan and took the wallet from him.

I flipped it open and saw the man that we were looking for. Brian Mercer looked to be in his late thirties, had neatly combed brown hair along with hazel eyes, and according to his wallet he was five foot seven.

"This was a great find. We finally know who we are hunting for." I said with joy. "Marcus what did you find?"

"I found these in the basement." Marcus said holding up pieces of paper that had been uncrumpled. "These were on a table near a trashcan. It seems that he was planning on burning them."

"What makes you think that?" I asked.

"There was a lot of ash in there. Seems that our killer likes to burn things." Marcus said.

"Have you read them?" I asked.

"Yup they are medical bills addressed to Brian." Marcus said. "It seems that our killer is sick."

"That might be what set him off and started all of this." I said.

"Did you find anything?" Ethan asked.

"I am going to show you what I found." I said as I drew my wand from my coat and aimed it at the bed. "Levo."

The bed began to float, and I moved it over by the dresser and looked at the wall that was the source of my issues.

"Are you going to break down the wall?" Ethan asked with resignation.

"No need. Revare Sectum." I said and we watched as the wall turned translucent revealing that behind the wall was a desk. "My friends it looks like we have found Bryan's secret alcove."

They could not see my expression, but I was smiling.

"Do you have a spell that can bring that desk over here?" Marcus asked.

"In a manner of speaking." I said as my left hand gripped my right arm and I stared at the wall with my right palm extended.

The stance was not needed but I wanted them to think that it took more effort. I apported the desk from behind the wall to the room with us.

"What do you think is on the inside?" Ethan asked.

"Let's find out." I said as I walked to the desk and opened the first drawer.

I hoped that I would find major secrets in there. If he was going to hide an entire desk in here, then it had to be very important to him.

The first drawer had the image of two rabbits kissing each other on a happy field.

"Adorable but completely useless." Marcus said.

The book was placed atop the desk. Hopefully the next drawer would have something better.

I opened the second drawer and found what looks to be a leather-bound journal. The journal is a black book. Bigger than a day planner but shorter than a notebook. There was a tassel passing through from a page somewhere in the middle.

Jenkins, it looks like we have found a clue.

"Yes." I cheered as I lifted the journal.

"What do you think is in it?" Marcus asked interested.

"Let's find out. This could be very useful. It could help us to understand how Bryan is finding his targets." I said as I moved to open it.

I was about to open the book when Marcus hit me with a rolled-up sock.

"Be careful. We are going after an evil wizard. If you open that you could fall into a trance." Marcus said.

"Very funny." I said rolling my eyes and picking up the book.

I flipped through the pages and saw that there was a lot written on the inside.

"How do you feel?" Marcus asked. "Are you getting the urge to kill roosters or write creepy messages in their blood?"

"No. Nor do I feel like setting a giant snake on unsuspecting school students." I said scowling.

"Fine but if you start feeling strange urges, I would like you to tell us." Marcus said. "At least so I have enough time to run away."

"Alright come on guys. We are now one step closer to ending all of this." Ethan said. "What is our next step?"

"I need to get what is in that journal inside of here." I said as I placed the journal on the desk and pulled out a notebook from my coat.

"Are you going to be doing this by hand?" Ethan asked.

"No. That would be ridiculous." I denied and pointed my wand at it. "Geminati."

The journal and the notebook began to glow white and when it finished an exact replica of the journal was next to it.

"Did you copy the entire content inside the journal?" Ethan asked.

"Yes." I said before picking up the copy and putting it away.

I put the journal back and apported it to its original position. I planned to come back for the original when everything was finished.

"Someone needs to watch the house for when he comes back here." Marcus said.

"Are you volunteering?" I asked.

"Not me." Marcus denied taking out his orange cellphone. "I was thinking that we could use our friends on the police force to come and keep an eye on the place."

"You want to use them as bait?" I asked horrified at the potential bloodbath. "They would stand no chance if he came back and found them."

"They don't need to wrap the house with crime scene tape. Just have a couple officers sit in a car on the street and alert us if anyone walks up to the door." Marcus said.

"His plan does make sense." Ethan said.

It was clear that I was outvoted.

"Very well but I want you to make sure that they stay in the car and don't try to confront him yet." I said.

"Okay, not a problem." Marcus said.

However, this plan did give me another idea that would help me figure out how to make sure that this case did not end up a mystery for the police to keep in an unsolved folder.

"Since we are going to use the police how about we give them the information that Marcus found in the basement." I said.

"You want them chasing the hospital lead?" Ethan asked.

"I told you that I don't want this becoming a cold case. That means the police are going to need a lead to chase. A motive to look for and a culprit to catch at the end of this." I explained.

All the things that I could give them.

"Sure." Marcus said shrugging.

"Time to go back." I said as I recalled Ethan into the necklace.

With that I moved to put the bed back to where it originally was.

"They are on their way." Marcus said when he was finished with his call.

"Come on." I said and put my hand on Marcus's shoulder.

Taking a deep breath, I teleported us downstairs and recreated the portal that would allow us to leave the house.

CHAPTER 15

"Hello detectives." Marcus said to them with a smile as they approached the street. "What's new with you?"

In my opinion there was no reason to make people angry until you had no other choice, or I felt that they deserved it. This is what I intended to keep Marcus around for. One person to annoy other people while I could be calm and peaceful. If we both stayed in our roles, then I had no doubt we could make this partnership work.

"Shouldn't the two of you would be helping Eddie find out who framed Roger?" Detective O'Connell asked.

"The Rabbit?" Marcus asked as he raised thumb and index finger to his chin. "I personally believe that it was the capitalist with the squeaky voice. I also believe that he is the one that killed Professor Pomegranate in the laundry room."

"I still feel like Mrs. Bluejay needs to be questioned further. Her alibi was suspect." I argued.

Detective Langdon clapped her hands. "I heard that you had a lead for us?"

"That is correct. The house we believe the killer owns is up the street." I said showing them a picture on my phone.

"How did you two find out about this place?" Detective O'Connell asked staring us down.

I could tell that if we didn't give him the right answer, he would try to arrest us for breaking and entering and obstructing justice. He wouldn't succeed but his attempt might have delayed us enough that Bryan managed to slip out through my fingers.

"The spirits led me here." I said. "After we found that grave, I heard words travelling through the wind. They are angry and are crying out for justice."

"The wind spoke to you?" Detective O'Connell asked with a raised eyebrow.

I could tell by his expression that he did not believe me. I wonder if to him we had neon signs that said frauds and suspicious.

"What did you manage to find after you broke into the house?" He questioned us.

He wouldn't get us that easily.

"That is a trick question." Marcus said. "Possible entrapment even."

"We weren't in the house. We were around the back looking for anything suspicious and then once we found something we were going to call you." I told him with a smile.

"Really?" Detective Langdon asked.

"That's right. I wanted to follow the lead, but Alex wanted us to keep you aware of everything that is happening." Marcus said.

"What did you find?" Detective Langdon asked.

"Here." I said holding up Bryan's medical bills.

"Did you do this?" Detective O'Connell asked looking at the paper. "Damaging evidence could also be considered obstruction."

"You just assume the worst about us." Marcus said as he placed his hand on his chest. "For a man with a comma to the top of his name that is just insulting."

"What does that matter?" I asked him curious about where he was going with it.

"I have heard that is god's comma." Marcus said.

"Who said that?" I asked.

"I've heard it on the streets." Marcus defended. "I once thought about changing my name so that is it M comma to the top Arcus."

"So, you want to be called M'arcus?" I asked, tilting my head. "Feels kind of weird."

"I plan to reinvent myself every decade. Keeps things interesting." Marcus said.

"It could be useful?"

"Useful how?" I asked.

"In case anyone decides to hunt me down in the future." Marcus said. "Most searches require spelling a person's name accurately."

"Can you two please focus? Where did you find this lead?" Detective Langdon asked.

Detective Langdon clapped her hands. "Can you two please focus? Where did you find this lead?"

"The spirits led us to the house. We walked around the fence looking for clues and when we came back, we found a trashcan that had been knocked to the ground." I said.

"The wind again?" Detective O'Connell asked.

"Or a racoon knocked it over. This is Philadelphia." I said with a shrug. "Anyway here."

"Hospital bills for Bryan Mercer?" Detective O'Connell asked me clearly curious and suspicious.

"We would like for you to and check it out." Marcus said to him.

"Why would we do that?" Detective O'Connell asked. "We have found five bodies in the park, and we have yet to identify who they are."

I had hoped that they would be interested enough to investigate it on their own, but it seems we would have to go with plan A.

"You misunderstand." Marcus said. "I want you to look into it for us."

I could hear the change in his tone.

"Yes. We will look into it." Detectives O'Connell and Langdon said in unison.

I felt happy even though I felt wary about doing this. Things were working out and soon we would catch Bryan. I should have known that the universe had let me have hope so I wouldn't suspect the fact that I might never live to see another sunrise again.

"I will call you for when you will go there but for now forget this part." Marcus said.

"Come on." I said as I walked to the car.

"You should have asked her out." Marcus said.

"Seriously?" I asked him as I opened the door.

"I know that you said that you had a problem with me using hypnotism on them so you should ask her yourself." Marcus said.

"I have plenty of time to ask her on a date when I am done hunting this killer." I said.

I pulled out the necklace and released Ethan.

"So, you convinced the police?" Ethan asked relaxing into the seat.

"Yep." I answered.

"Great." Ethan said. "Hey Marcus."

"Yeah?" Marcus asked turning from his window.

"I was wondering how did you walk inside the house?" Ethan asked.

"Did you gain amnesia during your time in the necklace?" Marcus asked. "Simple I walked through the blue glowing portal."

"So that whole thing about vampires needing invitation to houses is a lie?" Ethan asked.

"No, it is true that vampires need an invitation to enter a residence. The threshold acts as a barrier. The stronger they try to force it the harder the barrier pushes back against them." I answered him knowing Marcus wasn't going to.

He liked being mysterious and if a question would lessen his mystique or reveal a weakness, he would ignore it like it wasn't even asked. It annoyed me at times, so I tried to ruin it as much as possible when it wasn't inconvenient for me.

"What happens if a vampire were to walk inside a house, but they don't have an invitation?" Ethan asked.

"All I will say is that it does not end well." Marcus said looking away out the window.

What he was not saying was that if in the event that a vampire is not invited but is somehow brought inside a house they start to suffocate and bleed from their eyes until they either leave or die.

"Then how did you get inside without suffering?" Ethan asked.

"Marcus has already had almost every homeowner in this city that isn't supernatural hypnotized to let him in and so Bryan was probably only renting that house." I told him.

"Isn't that a little much?" Ethan asked like a sensible person.

While that was true for other people, for Marcus that was his level of normal. Being a vampire was known to amplify all their feelings and emotions. It was the first thing written down in textbooks on them.

"Not by my standards." Marcus denied. "It is not even the craziest thing I have ever done."

"What do you mean?" Ethan asked.

"One of the things I did in my first year as a vampire was that I hunted down everyone I ever went to school with." Marcus told him with an ominous tone.

I looked up to the reflection of the mirror and could see a grin on his face.

"Why did you do that?" Ethan asked clearly regretting asking the question.

"Why did I hunt them down?" Marcus asked, enjoying every second of this to build suspense.

"Yes." Ethan said hesitant but seemingly determined to continue forward.

"I hunted my classmates so that I could erase every embarrassing moment of me from their minds." Marcus said.

"Is that all that you did to them?" Ethan asked hesitantly.

"Did you think that I killed them? Man, Alex was right. You are grim." Marcus said turning to him as his face went back to normal while he acted like he did not try to sound suspicious on purpose. "Were you like this when you were alive?"

I was also surprised by the fact that removing embarrassing memories was the only thing he did. I feared for the day when Marcus decided to act out on his more ridiculous ideas.

So many Hollywood celebrities were going to find themselves stranded in the desert with nothing but a compass and a map with no idea how they got there. If they managed to get home, they would learn that before they left, that they had sent vast amounts of the money that they spent on mansions and villas in foreign countries to charities and hospitals.

Ethan opened and closed his mouth before he looked out the window. I have no idea what he was thinking but I could tell that the spirit was clearly annoyed.

"What information do you think the journal has?" Marcus asked me as I took the turn to head back to my office.

"I believe that it will list the type of spells he prefers and the ritual he is using in his murders." I said. "Hopefully it will also tell us what the sigils mean."

"Now that we know more what do you think his end goal might be?" Ethan asked.

"From what I glimpsed in the journal and the ritual circle in the warehouse it seems that he is trying to extend his lifespan." I said. "Maybe even become immortal."

That could not be allowed to happen.

"Aren't most of you wizards immortal?" Ethan questioned me. "You said your teacher managed it."

"That is not what I said. I said there are some." I corrected him. "I think there are probably enough to fill about a public- school classroom."

"Do you think you can figure out where he learned his spells?" He asked.

I sighed at his question. "Saying that out loud is way easier than actually doing it."

"What do you mean?" Ethan asked.

"There are many magic schools that were developed to teach magic and share knowledge. The languages they use vary from school to school. Searching through them would take time." I told him while trying to put all the pieces together in a way that fit the puzzle we were dealing with.

"Magic schools?" Ethan questioned me. "Are the school like Hogwarts or is it more like Brakebills? Were there magic stairs constantly shifting to different platforms?"

I gave a half and half shrug. I knew what he was referencing but I could not give an answer more precise.

"How do you not know?" Ethan asked.

"I was home-schooled in magic." I said. "Anyway, it seems that we have gotten off topic. We need to focus on Bryan's goal and the people he has been killing."

"So how many lives do you think he plans on taking before this is over?" Marcus asked.

"It depends on the gains he is getting from the murder." I said as we parked right outside of the office. "However even one more life taken to feed him is too much."

"While we are on morbid topics Ethan Alex has something to tell you." Marcus said.

I gripped the car wheel and glared at him through the rearview mirror.

Marcus, seeing the look on my face quickly got out of the car and used his speed to be as far from the car as possible.

Not only did he spook the kid, but he also made this even more awkward. I calmed down with a sigh. It was my fault for believing that I would have more time to deal with this.

"Ethan Marcus is right there is something I have got to tell you." I said.

"Yeah, what is it?" Ethan asked.

I really wished that something would happen that would interrupt me from finishing what I had to say. Nothing came and so I decided to rip the band aid right off, trying to be as quick as possible.

"Your aunt's missing." I said, wincing as I finished.

He took a deep breath before he nodded, however, I noticed that his fingers were beginning to clench.

"You thought something like this would happen?" I asked him.

"My Aunt wasn't well. I'm guessing you saw her?" He questioned me.

I nodded. "I thought she was close to having a breakdown."

"I was her last living relative. My parents were in Chicago on a work trip, and they died when some nutjob opened fire in the shopping area. She never married as she was rather shy. She is sweet and caring but could freak out rather easily. With me missing…"

He didn't finish but it was clear what might have happened to her and if not that there were plenty of creatures that would find her misery enticing.

Not all of them supernatural.

I had lost my parents but that was a while ago and I could call them whenever I needed to.

"Do you want to talk about it?" I asked him.

It was difficult for me to say the sentence. Not just because of the awkward atmosphere but because I could remember what it was like after I lost my parents. The false sympathy offered by strangers just made me angrier. They offered their sympathies and platitudes, but they did not understand nor wanted me to bum them out with how I really felt.

"No." Ethan said. "Can you just give me some time to think?"

"Sure." I said as I gave him a nod and got out the car.

I was given an out and I was not going to waste it. I looked at the dark sky above and counted the seconds as they passed.

My eyes moved when I noticed him passing through the door. "How are you feeling?"

"I am still determined to find the person that killed me, but I also ask that you try your best to find my aunt." He said.

"I will do my best." I said and brought him back into the necklace.

I locked the car and headed inside my office to start reading the journal.

CHAPTER 16

"How far did you get?" Ethan asked as he walked from the back room.

I had been sitting at my desk minding my own business and eating the bagels that I would have for dinner. His appearance surprised me and that had me jumping up and dropping my food.

"I thought you were watching television." I said with annoyance when I noticed that my bagel had rolled off of my desk and fallen to the ground.

"I got bored of that, so I decided to check on you." Ethan said. "Have you read the journal? Or have you been too busy eating?"

"Yes, I have read the journal." I said scowling. "I am just taking a short break right now."

I had to stop short of telling him that I had to eat given his current circumstances. It would just be hurtful and unnecessary.

"Alright then what have you learned?" Ethan asked gesturing at the copied journal at the desk. "Does the journal mention who he is going to target next?"

"To begin with I have learned that the journal we took is something his therapist recommended to keep track of his feelings during the day." I said.

"Clearly they are charging more than they are worth." Ethan said. "Are we going to pay them a visit?"

"No." I denied. "I had Marcus look into it. It seems that he has stopped seeing her but thankfully he has decided to keep the journal."

I lifted the book and turned it to the page I had paused at. The passage was seven months old and probably when he first began his murder spree.

"Well, I also have learned that Bryan wasn't publicly trained in magic." I said as I read the page again. "In fact, if I had met him a year ago, he would have had no idea that magic even existed."

"How is that possible?" Ethan asked. "What about the warehouse?"

"One day when he was coming from the hospital that he met a person who told him that magic could cure him." I said. "Our earlier guess was right. Apparently, Bryan has or had a deadly disease that is incurable by modern science. For the past two years he had been feeling worse as the days passed. His arms were getting weaker, his vision was growing dimmer, and from time to time his legs would give out on him."

"So, he figured since science could not help him, he would turn to magic for a cure. No matter what it cost." Ethan said.

I turned to an earlier page.

"I finally found a way to become immortal, the answer is Sacrificial magic. With this I can finally have everything that I want, and I will never have to die!" I quoted as I performed what I believed to be a rather accurate imitation of Bryan.

I had seen a page before this one and it had been littered with symbols. According to the notes they caused age suspension magic when placed on a person's skin. I assume that Bryan had gotten them tattooed onto his body to keep his sickness from advancing while he learned.

It was obvious and understandable why he would try to add years to his lifespan but even if I could understand his reason, it did not mean that I accepted his methods, nor would I be able to forgive him for all that he put me through.

"Even in his writing he sounds insane." Ethan said scornfully.

"He is sick and that has led him to desperation." I said.

"Are you trying to ignore what he has done to his victims?" Ethan asked with anger in his voice. "The people he has hurt in his effort to try and cure his body."

"No." I denied with a shake of the head. "Just because I can understand his pain does not mean I believe that he should get away with this."

"Let's move past this topic." Ethan said. "Do you know what type of sacrificial ritual he is using?"

"Yes. The magic that Bryan is using is an old sacrificial type called Legaal's Tenebris Donum." I said solemnly while glaring at the wall. "Apparently Bryan's teacher gave him the books that he would need to walk down this path."

Just imagining the sort of person that would do this made me want to break something.

"Is that a big deal?" Ethan asked.

It was not a surprise that was his reaction. He had no idea what I was talking about given that he only recently learned about magic, so he didn't get the importance and the dangers of this.

"Sacrificial magic is a banned magical practice." I told him. "It requires power from sacrifice like the name implies and while most of the time it has come from animals there is always one group or another that decides to use intelligent beings to gain their results."

I always thought that it was ironic given since you aren't sacrificing anything you actually care about but the lives of other things.

"Really I thought you wizards were the type to sacrifice animals in your potions and spells." Ethan said. "Sacrificing the wool of a sheep for thicker hair or the eyes of a snake to detect body heat."

"That is stereotyping, and it is wrong." I countered. "Anyway, using dead animal parts in rituals is a completely separate thing. The council of magic made it known that practicing this type of magic carried a sentence of multiples of ten years based on the scale and number of the sacrifice. When Bryan is caught and brought to trial he would be sentenced to prison for a very long time."

The fact of the matter was the world was entering the age of enlightenment. The world was changing, and the council wanted to take advantage of it. The council had been created just a decade earlier and the idea to create the Alter-plane began to gain favor with the wizards/witches in the world.

"So, as they had agreed to let magic become a less obvious fact of this world styles of magic were lost, destroyed, and banned. Places were created to store all that information and then they were sealed so that no one could use that type of magic ever again." I said.

"Isn't that an overreaction?" Ethan asked.

"In some ways I agree. In others it was the wiser choice. Sacrificial magic requires power from a living sacrifice like the name implies and while most of the time it has come from animals there is always one group or another that decides to use intelligent beings to gain their results." I said.

It helped to put an end to those ancient stories of wizards/witches kidnapping people in the woods to eat them and strange cults sacrificing villages.

Nowadays if that happened it was just assumed that it was a crazy person or satanists.

"Do you know how he has been picking his targets?" Ethan asked glaring at the journal. "What did we ever do to this bastard?"

"Yes." I answered. "When you were alive had you recently visited the hospital in the past few months?"

"Yeah. To get my cast off. I broke my arm in a skateboarding accident." Ethan answered stretching out his right arm. "Why?"

"That is how he found you and the others." I answered him scowling as I recalled his motivation. "Ever since Bryan found himself sick, he had spent time in the hospital watching people come and go. After he decided that he was going to hunt people for his rituals he decided to use people that he saw coming out of hospitals with happy looks on their faces. He thinks that it was unfair that he was dying while you were walking out with smiles on your faces."

"How many people has he killed?" Ethan asked.

"I believe that you were his nineteenth kill." I answered grimly as I thought of all the people yet to be found.

"That many?" Ethan asked. "So, he should not need to kill anymore?"

If only the universe was so kind. At least we had places to search for the identities of Bryan's victims. He had kept notes on which hospitals his targets had come from.

"It is worse than you think." I said with a sigh. "If he had been planning to just use the ritual to gain life force, he only needed one victim and that would have lasted decades. It seems that he has also been using your life force to gather power and unfortunately, it seems that the powerup is indeed permanent."

"What does that mean?" Ethan asked. "What is he planning on doing with the years that he stole from us?"

"It means that all of his murders have been preparation work. A portion is going to healing his body, but he is using the majority of your life force to increase his power. The weapon that he murdered you with is being used as both medium for the ritual and as his focus."

Which explained why Ethan's wound radiated dark magic. Each murder would taint the blade further.

"What does that mean?" Ethan asked.

"After we capture Bryan, the weapon will have to be destroyed." I answered. "After all the evil Bryan has performed anyone that might come into contact risk the dangers of being corrupted."

"The blade is cursed?" Ethan asked.

"Correct." I answered.

There was even worse news.

His power was growing with each death like a hamster running through a wheel for a sunflower seed. As long as that hamster kept running more power would be generated.

"Why is he doing this if his goal is to be cured of his disease and live a longer life?" Ethan asked.

"Because he does not want a longer life. He wants immortality." I answered him. "The problem is what happens if he gets him though. As an immortal he would forever be out of our reach. The council would not lift a finger to help us catch him. They would wave him off and that would probably be the last we ever saw of him."

"There is no way that we can allow that to happen." Ethan said glaring in frustration with his fingers starting to clench.

"I do not intend to let it." I said and turned to the last page in his journal. "He has decided to plant the flag on his sandcastle of murder. His next target is Geoffrey Keller."

On the page was an image of Geoffrey. He is Caucasian with brown hair the color of sand. In the picture his eyes were hidden behind shades, so they remained a mystery. He looked to be in his late twenties to early thirties.

"Are we too late to stop him?" Ethan questioned me.

"No. According to his journal he is planning to go after him on Friday." I answered him.

That left us with three days to stop him.

"What is so special about him that you refer to him as the flag?" Ethan asked.

"Geoffrey Keller is a vampire." I answered.

"There were no other supernatural creatures on the list of people that he targeted?" Ethan asked.

"Beings. Supernatural creatures are things cannot think or talk." I corrected. "As for your question No. No, there were no other supernatural beings on the list."

"Then why is he going after a vampire?" Ethan asked.

"This is who he has been targeting since he learned of magic, He wants the healing power and immortality that a vampire offers." I said. "After he gathers enough power, he plans to use the ritual to connect the two of them so that he never has to worry about dying again."

An endless resource to draw energy and power from.

"Do you have a way to track Geoffrey?" Ethan asked.

"Unfortunately, not. It seems that we will have to use Bryan's information and hope that we get to him first." I said.

"Are you going to call Marcus so we can come up with a plan?" Ethan asked.

"That is a job for tomorrow." I told him with a smile.

Even with the difficulties it seemed like everything was in the bag. We knew Bryan's target and where he would be. We had police officers watching Bryan's house. We had three days to prepare what we wanted to say and come up with a plan.

All we had to do was keep the two of them from meeting and we would be able to ruin his plans.

I had no idea the danger I was putting myself in by hunting down Geoffrey Keller and how much pain I would be put through.

CHAPTER 17

"Has everything been set up?" I asked Marcus as I walked to the bench near the entrance of the Banneker hospital and looked at the building.

It is an eight-storied building that reached into the sky like a hand. The entrance was covered by a red awning. The automatic doors opened with a clear whoosh as people walked through.

I was tempted to go and buy a snack from the corner store right next to it, but I had to stay where I was and wait for the detectives to come.

"Yes. when I visited earlier, I made sure that the moment the police ask to see Bryan's doctor that Sheila will lead them to her." Marcus answered.

"You learned the receptionist's name?" I asked surprised.

"Of course. I am a people person. I try to learn the name of everyone that I interact with." Marcus bragged. "Lovely lady. She has been divorced twice but still believes in the idea of love. Her sister Janice is getting married in the summer."

"Great for her." I said with a sigh as I sat on the bench and looked at the Seven-Eleven.

I wondered if they sold ice cream sandwiches.

"You are going to have to slip her a twenty to activate the command." Marcus said.

"Seriously?" I asked as I looked at my phone. "Why would you do that?"

"I figured that if we are setting all of this up then we might as well go all the way." Marcus said laughing. "You should be happy that I did not make you wait outside with a suitcase of money and a secret password."

"I want you to know that I am flipping you off." I said then shook my head and regained focus. "Which doctor are we going to meet?"

"Her name is Dr. Shakkar." Marcus answered. "According to Sheila she is the last doctor that Bryan visited here before he started killing."

"Have you prepared her story?" I asked.

"Yeah. The problem is that she is not going to tell you anything." Marcus said.

"What? That was the whole point of having the detectives come here to question her. We went over this yesterday." I said in an angry whisper wishing that I had more magic power so I could apportate weapons beyond my line of sight and across town.

We had agreed to split up the work. I would watch over the detectives and make sure that they learned what they needed to while Marcus and Ethan watched over the nightclub that Geoffrey was supposed to appear at. They would check the entrance and any possible exits where somebody could be ambushed at.

This was supposed to be over and done with by the end of the day. So that we would be ready when Geoffrey arrived at the club tomorrow. We had spent hours discussing how it would work and he wanted to change the plan without telling anyone.

Marcus knew that was one of the easiest ways to make me angry.

"Wow. I can feel your glare over the phone." Marcus said. "Relax. I just decided it was better to give Dr. Shakkar a nurse to help sell the story."

"Why?" I asked while feeling the urge to look up to the sky and start shouting.

"Doctors are trained to act cool and composed under pressure. I figured if we wanted the story to seem true, we should use someone more emotional." Marcus said. "Someone like a nurse."

"Are you going to tell me what she is going to say?" I asked worried how long that this might take.

"I would prefer it to be a surprise." Marcus denied.

"Very well. How am I going to activate her story?" I asked already giving in to playing his game.

"Dr. Shakkar is going to ask for one of the detectives to ask for a badge and when they show her it will start." Marcus answered. "However, they will get nowhere with her, and it will be your job to lead them to the nurse."

At least that won't cost me money.

"What is the nurse going to do?" I asked.

"Dr. Shakkar will leave the room first and then Nurse Ramirez will begin." Marcus said.

A car driving near the entrance gained my attention before I noticed who was inside.

"Alright. Wait. I think that I see them coming." I said as I looked over my shoulder.

"Really? Out in public? How indecent." Marcus said laughing. "Do you think that we should call the police chief and get them arrested for public indecency?"

"Very funny." I said hanging up the phone before he could try and tell another dirty joke.

I watched as they walked out of the car and to the entrance.

"Hello, Detective Langdon, it is nice to see you again." I said then lowered my newspaper with a faux smile. "Detective O'Connell."

That greeting, though polite, was given with less warmth.

The beautiful Detective Langdon turned towards me in surprise.

"What are you doing here?" Detective Langdon asked.

"I wanted to make sure that you and your angry partner found the right doctor to talk to in this place." I said looking at the two doors that would lead to the reception desk.

"Did the wind by chance tell you who that was?" Detective O'Connell asked scornfully.

"Yes, they did but I knew I would need a police badge to get them to talk." I said standing up. "So, shall we work together?"

"I would hate nothing more." Detective O'Connell said.

"Come on. I led you to this lead." I said. "Would it not be better that we work together?"

"We are trained detectives. What could we possibly need from a psychic?" Detective O'Connell asked.

"That is hurtful." I said and turned to Detective Langdon "Do you feel the same way?"

"I have to agree." Detective Langdon declined politely. "I just don't see any way that you could do what we could not."

"A way in." I said as I stood in front of them. "You could spend hours waiting for the doctor that you are looking for or you could go with me and take a direct line to the doctor."

"Really?" Detective Langdon asked.

"Plus, you can't talk to a doctor about a patient without their permission." I argued. "I however am not a detective and can get her to imply things that you can use later."

I did not intend to let it go that far. The plan was for the duplicate of Bryan Mercer to suffer a heart attack during his interrogation. The police may never get the answers that they wanted but it would close the case.

"We are only allowing this because we have someone burying dead bodies." Detective O'Connell said.

"Great." I said with a smile. "I hope one day we can have a relationship like Batman and Police Chief Gordan. Or at least Detective Bullock."

Detective O'Connell just glared and walked off. The automatic doors shutting closely behind with a whooshing sound.

"Did I say something?" I asked Detective Langdon.

"He does not approve of vigilantes." Detective Langdon asked as she shook her head.

"He hates superheroes?" I asked watching him through the doors and walk straight to the reception desk.

"Ever since he was a child." Detective Langdon said. "He hates the ideas of costume vigilantes doing police work. Almost as much as psychic consultants."

"Such a shame." I said as I shook my head.

"Where is your lawyer?" Detective Langdon asked.

Lawyer? Oh, right Marcus. That was the excuse that we gave to them to get me out of interrogation.

"He is busy with something else at the moment." I said as the doors opened, and we walked in.

The hospital had a rather dry atmosphere. The reception area had a smell of antiseptic and bleach that hung in the air. I could look down and see that the carpet had been vacuumed recently but the heat of the machine had been gone for a while. People sat down focused on their phones or one of the magazine that had been taken from a table.

"Should we do something?" I asked while watching Detective O'Connell stand near the end of the line. "It seems that he might be close to erupting."

"You are the one that set him off." Detective Langdon said.

"Which is why I have to be the one to do something to make it right." I said as I walked past the line and to the side.

I ignored the people calling out to me with insults.

The receptionist at the desk had a bleached white shirt that contrasted with her dark skin and blonde hair.

"Hello Sheila." I said with a smile.

Sheila popped her gum. "Do I know you?"

"I am Alex Blackwell. I am a psychic detective working with the Philadelpha police." I said and slid the folded up twenty-dollar bill in front of her.

Her eyes glanced at it, and I watched as her eyes began to dim.

"Really?" Sheila asked.

"I can prove it." I said as I placed my right hand over my eyes and pointed at her with the first two fingers on my left. "You have a sister named Janice."

"Yes, I do." Sheila confirmed.

"The spirits are telling me that she is getting married in the summer." I said.

"Wow. That's right." Sheila said as she slammed her hands on the table.

"Now would you mind answering some of my friend's questions?" I asked with a smile.

"No problem." Sheila said.

"You can ask her now." I said to Detective Langdon.

"We are looking for on information on a man named Bryan Mercer." Detective Langdon said. "We believe that he has visited this hospital two years ago."

"The spirits have told me that he was a patient of Dr. Shakkar." I "informed" her.

"The spirits?" Dr. Shakkar asked.

"Don't get him started." Detective O'Connell said shaking his head.

"Give me a moment and I will check if she is free." Sheila said.

"Please and thank you." I said with a smile as I moved back from the reception desk.

"How did you know that about her sister?" Detective Langdon asked.

"I told you that I have a gift." I said as I took a seat and pulled out my newspaper. "You can inform your partner that he can come and join us."

The newspaper hid my grin as I watched the detective walk away.

"Langdon said that you have gotten the attendant to give you an answer." Detective O'Connell said grudgingly.

"All it takes is the right approach and a smile." I said as I looked at the reception desk. Sheila gestured for us to come to her.

"Looks like our receptionist has found our doctor." I said as I stood up and walked to the reception desk. "Hello again."

"Dr. Shakkar is in room 312 waiting for you." Sheila said.

"Thank you." I said as I pushed off of the table and turned to the detectives. "Let's go."

We moved past the wooden fence blocking our way and walked to the elevator.

"Do you want to lead into this or should I?" I asked, turning to them after I pressed the third-floor button.

"You are the one who volunteered to come." Detective O'Connell said. I will take that as a sign of his approval.

"I think that one day we will be good friends." I said, giving him a smile and a thumbs up.

Marcus would have made some joke or tried to insult him as a response to his actions but that would not be my step. I would appear to try my hardest to be his friend. I knew that it would annoy him the most.

He hated my positivity even more and he turned away from me.

"Can we try and work together here?" Detective Langdon asked.

"I would rather have my thumb get stabbed with a fishing pole hook again." Detective O'Connell muttered.

If it happens more than once maybe fishing is not the sport for you. The doors opened behind us.

"Let's go!" I cheered as I led us to the room that Dr. Shakkar was waiting for us in.

The room was rather simple. It had an examination table connected to the wall covered by a plastic sheet, a container for disposable waste and a few motivational posters meant to cheer people up.

"Can I help you?" Dr. Shakkar asked as she turned towards them.

Dr. Shakkar looked to be in her forties. She had brown skin that led me to believe she was of Indian descent. Her dark hair was tied into a ponytail that reached down the back of her doctor's coat.

The nurse with her had tan skin and her hair was dyed a bright red.

"I am Alex Blackwell. The two behind me are police detectives and they wish to talk to you about Bryan Mercer." I said introducing myself with a quick bow.

"Can I see your badges?" Dr. Shakkar asked. I fought the urge to smile.

"Here." Detectives Langdon and O'Connell said as they showed her their badges.

"What can you tell us about Bryan Mercer?" Detective O'Connell said. "When was the last time that you remember seeing him?"

"I cannot tell you much, but I will tell you that he was rather angry the last time that I saw him." Dr. Shakkar said.

"Because of his disease?" I asked.

"I cannot answer that." Dr. Shakkar said shaking her head.

"Fine. We already knew that he was sick. His medical bills led us here." I said. "The spirits have also told me that he grew rather angry when he learned his issue could not be fixed with modern medicine."

"I cannot confirm whether that is true." Dr. Shakkar said neither confirming nor denying. "After hearing my review on his results, he soon left the room and exited the building."

"Fine. Nurse Ramirez, can you tell me what you remember of Mr. Mercer?" I asked turning to her.

Nurse Ramirez jumped in surprise "Me?"

"I get the feeling that you saw him one more time." I said pointing at her.

"Yes, I saw him when I was on my lunch break." Nurse Ramirez said. "He was sitting on the bench so still that I thought that he was deep in thought."

"You went to go check on him." I said.

"Yes. I did." Nurse Ramirez answered uncomfortably.

"What happened next?" I asked.

"I went to see how he was doing." Nurse Ramirez answered.

"You should not have done that." Dr. Shakkar said shaking her head. "You should have contacted security and let them handle it."

"Were you afraid that he could be dangerous?" I asked.

It would be good for the detectives to believe that he had anger issues.

"It is not a rare thing that happens with people that visit hospitals. Some get sad. Others get angry." Dr. Shakkar said. "There are protocols in place to make sure that the response is handled properly."

"How angry did he get?" I asked, turning back to Nurse Ramirez. "Did you ever think that he was going to attack you?"

"It was more the look in his eyes when I approached him." Nurse Ramirez said as she started shaking and moved to place her hand on the mattress. "The rage in them caught me off guard."

"Are you okay?" Detective Langdon asked, placing a hand on her shoulder.

"I will be." Nurse Ramirez said. "Still, I asked him if he needed me to call someone. He declined my offer and walked away."

"He has not been back since?" I asked.

"He called the hospital to inform us that he wasn't coming back." Dr. Shakkar said. "He told us that he decided he would be turning to non- traditional medicine from that point on."

"Really?" Detective Langdon asked surprised.

"The spirits have told me that he has reached a point where he is desperate for anything that can help him." I informed them.

"I have told you all that I know. If you don't mind, I have a patient to treat and I will need my nurse's assistance." Detective Shakkar said as she moved to walk out of the room.

"Very well." Detective Langdon said handing out her card. "Call if you remember anything else."

We walked in silence to the elevator.

"I think today was rather productive." I said, pulling my right hand out of my coat and pressed the button to send us back down to the lobby. "What about you two?"

"I am starting to think Bryan is our guy." Detective O'Connell admitted. "At least enough to have a warning about the guy put out."

"It's like you read my mind." I said with a smile.

I walked out first to let them have the chance to discuss what they had learned.

"Marcus I have to admit that your story has worked." I said as I walked out of the hospital and to my car.

Now that they had the motive behind Bryan's murders it was time to prepare to catch him. Tomorrow we would strike, and Bryan would be arrested.

At the time I should have worried that the gray clouds drifting in the sky above me could have been an ill omen for what was to come.

CHAPTER 18

Catching my reflection in the mirror I gave a sigh at what I was forced to wear. We were headed to a nightclub called Blood Moon. We had to blend in with our environment and that meant changing my clothes.

That meant I had been forced to leave my trench coat back at the office along with my wand and other magic items. I was now wearing an outfit that made me look like I just came from a music video from the nineteen-nineties. I was wearing a puffy dress shirt with a black vest over it and black pants and shoes.

In his Journal Bryan wrote that Geoffrey always arrived at the club at eleven. We had decided that we would arrive two hours early and make sure that our plan would work and that we would not face an unexpected surprise.

That had been the hope anyway. Given the position I am in now clearly things had not turned out as well as we hoped.

I had a scowl on my face as I walked into the car and turned it on. The sky was dark and there was a cold wind blowing through the streets and sending chills down my back.

"Calm down. It is just a nightclub." Marcus said as he stood outside the car.

I was really just glad he had picked something normal. The last time he had helped me with a case he had been wearing an Elvis Presley outfit and it took a lot of work for me to ignore that. This time he is wearing a short black T- shirt that reached his elbows and black jeans.

"What do you mean?" I asked with a hopefully reassuring smile.

"I can hear you gripping that wheel like its Halloween candy about to be stolen by a bully." Marcus said as he got in the car.

"Given what we might be up against I figure it makes sense to be concerned." Ethan argued.

"That might be true if he was worried about fighting the dark wizard." Marcus said shaking his head. "He is worried about something else."

"What do you mean?" Ethan asked. "I thought the police detectives bought your story?"

"I am worried about stepping foot in Blood Moon." I answered. "Night clubs are filled with loud music and drunk people. I prefer something less likely to cause me a migraine and lash out in annoyance."

"However, annoying you find it to be you are the one that roped us into this so there is no way that you could possibly back out." Marcus said.

"I know so all of that so you can save the lecture." I said reluctantly as I started turning the car.

Doing the right thing meant that sometimes you had to suffer through hard times. Doing things, you didn't like doing even when they moved you out of your comfort zone and into a place of chaos and fear. That created a situation that fueled the nightmares that you knew would torment you at night.

I counted to five to center myself. I had to be calm and composed but knowing our destination that was almost impossible.

Acting like a mature and reasonable adult was annoying.

"Fine let's go over what we know and the plan again." I said after taking a deep breath.

"Seriously?" Ethan asked. "We spent all of Wednesday going over the plan."

"Since Marcus wants to change plans on the fly, I want to make sure that we know what is happening and why." I said leaning my head back trying to get comfortable.

Anything to distract me from my fears and discomforts.

"Bryan is after a vampire to sacrifice." Ethan said.

"And as the only vampire in the group I also want to ask for hazard pay." Marcus joked. "If we ruin his plans he may decide to come after me as the sacrifice."

"Bryan plans to capture Geoffrey at the Blood Moon so that he can perform a ritual and gain a vampire's immortality." I continued.

"He has gone through so much effort when he could just become a vampire and gain immortality." Ethan muttered with disdain.

The reason behind that decision was obvious for any wizard or witch but as I was the only one in the group, so I had to be the one to explain.

"The Hybrid Effect." I told them. "When vampires try to turn supernatural beings, it is only a one in ten chance that they keep their old abilities and become hybrids. So, to my people it is not worth the risk."

"Really?" Ethan asked. "So, when it comes immortality if the price is giving up your magic you would turn away?"

"The ideal version of immortality for a wizard/witch is basically to have a body that could not age or die with a limitless supply of magic power." I said.

"That makes it seem that the desire of wizards and witches is to become a god." Ethan said.

"It would not surprise me." Marcus said. "Spending decades hovering over tomes in musty towers has to have a purpose besides being able to grow a long white beard."

He may be making fun of my culture, but he was not wrong.

"It is the promised end result of all our research and experiments." I said.

"All of it started by a desire for power and driven by ego." Marcus said.

"Bryan had little magic power to start with. He has murdered his way to build up the power to take down Geoffrey." I said turning back on topic as I turned the car to the right. "We won't let that happen. Now once we arrive at Blood Moon what will we do?"

"We split up." Ethan answered. "I will stay behind in the car to warn you if Bryan arrives."

"Correct and if he does arrive do not enter the club. I want you to call us on the prepaid phone that I gave you." I said, turning to look in the side mirror and turning left. "Marcus?"

"You and I will go in the club. You will sit at the bar and watch as I approach Geoffrey and try to convince him of the threat." Marcus said.

It was probably better that Geoffrey was warned by a fellow vampire. No one would find his approach suspicious.

The Blood Moon is a club that served as a way to feed vampires. They could drink and dance as they picked the unsuspecting person that they wanted for the night. According to the information Marcus found out vampires paid the club owner money, and they are given a chip. That chip signified that they could point out any human in the club claim them. Any others interested would have to find someone else or request that they could share.

After the humans have been fed on, they are sent to the bar to be given food and drink to replenish the blood that they lost. When the humans leave, they are hypnotized to come back the next time that they want to party and bring friends. They didn't exclude anybody. The only restriction for the humans that venture inside is that they are of age.

It sounded dangerous and I doubted that everyone that walked into that club would walk out alive. There was probably a time that vampires got too overzealous with their "food" and drained them dry.

"If he listens, I will contact Ethan so he can drive the car to the meeting point." I continued.

"Then we use our vampire speed to leave the club through the back alley and ger to the car and drive to the office." Marcus finished.

"Then while we keep Geoffrey hidden and safe, we can scry for Bryan's hiding place and take him down." I said glaring at the road.

"Let's hope that keeping things simple helps us." Ethan said.

"We're here." I said as I parked the car. "Good luck."

I got out of the car and listened as Ethan locked the doors.

Marcus and I walked right up to the entrance and not even three minutes later had we run into our first challenge.

The guy had dark skin and even darker shades to hide his eyes. He was tall, about six foot and muscled too. I already didn't like him due to the fact that he was taller than me but the scowl he aimed at me when I walked up led me to believe that we weren't going to get along.

"Move along kid you have to be twenty-one to enter." The bouncer said with a deep voice blocking the entrance with his body and stretching his arm out in front of me.

Times like this the fact that I looked to be nineteen was incredibly unhelpful.

"Look." I said I showed him my I.D. "I am twenty-three."

"That is a good fake. Better than the ones I see most of the time." The bouncer taunted me.

He was probably prepared to use force to make me leave if I didn't get the message.

If I had been in a better mood, I might have tried to bribe him to let me through but tonight I was in a hurry. I took several steps back glancing at the empty street and alleyway just to be sure. There was a smile on my face when for witnesses and smiled when I saw none. I raised my right hand and put pressure on the bouncer while lifting him a few centimeters off of the ground.

Telekinesis was another skill I learned. I usually used my wand to aim and keep the target steady, but I had more than enough skill for this. He did not take that well and it was even worse when I used it again to bring his sunglasses to my face.

"Wizard." He growled at me with his eyes changing color and his fangs descending.

"Yes. Now let me in or you are going to be tossed halfway across the city." I said smiling and pointing at him with my pointer and index finger extended.

I could feel it as he tried to use his supernatural strength to break free. There was no way that I was going to allow that to happen and so I started using more power.

"When I get free, I will rip your heart out." The bouncer growled.

There was a quick snap of his neck and his body fell to the ground.

"I could tell that this was going to take a while." Marcus said kicking the bouncer in the stomach and flipping him over. "This way was faster."

"I am not going to complain." I commented with a grin on my face to Marcus who just shrugged. "How long do you think he is going to be out?"

"He'll wake up in like twenty minutes with only a headache." Marcus said. "Come help me move him to the alley."

We lifted the vampire bouncer to the alley by the club and set his body down by the wall. I watched as Marcus stole the money from his wallet and his silver watch.

"You really had to steal from him?" I questioned him.

He nodded.

"Other vampires would kill him for getting in their way. So, the way I see it is being robbed is a much kinder act." Marcus said as he put the wallet back in the bouncer's pocket and began walking off with a whistle.

I thought he sounded like a tea kettle that was telling you it was done.

As I looked at the bouncer's body I sighed and tossed his shades onto his body.

Now with nobody blocking our way any longer we entered the club. I wished to cover my ears and drown out the sound of the music so I could hear myself think. Looking around I could see people dancing on the floor and above them were people that were hanging around in booths and tables either trying to look important or those having fun with friends or a combination of both.

"Have some fun. I am going to go blend." Marcus said as he walked to the dance floor.

Even after my lecture in the car he went and changed the plan.

"I should have known that this was going to happen." I said shaking my head as I walked to the bar. I intended to get more information.

Since Geoffrey is a regular here, there would probably be someone who knew him and where he sat. I knew the quickest way to find those answers people would be from the people serving drinks to the tables. as I walked to the bar, I wondered why the universe wanted to cause me such pain. I worked hard and did the right thing, why couldn't it just let me be happy and let me stay in my happy place.

Instead, I was here in a place that I would have avoided my entire life if I was able.

Before I could say anything though the bartender picked up an empty bottle and walked through the door behind him. Another bit of information that Marcus told me is that as a method of keeping the humans coming here the drinks are one-third the price they would be in any other bar in the city.

I took a seat by the counter waiting for the bartender to come back. After ten minutes passed, I gave a sigh and began tapping my fingers against the table.

How long did it take to find a replacement bottle?

"I thought I recognized you. You are that psychic detective?" A voice said with a happy tone of voice.

I turned toward the speaker.

He was five foot eight, He had brown hair and hazel eyes, and he was wearing a white-collar shirt and black jacket and pants.

"How do you know me?" I asked, trying to remember if this guy had been a client.

"I'm Michael, I saw you and those detectives at Banneker hospital." Michael said.

"I'm fine. I am just looking for somebody that owes child support." I lied to him as I tried to turn back to the bar.

"Who are you looking for?" Michael offered as he took a seat next to me. "Maybe I can help you."

"Why do you care?" I asked suspiciously.

"It would be a cool story to tell my friends during a barbeque." Michael said with a shrug. "Anyway, if you want to be heard over the music in a place like this you need to be able to yell."

I took a deep breath and was about to tell the guy that I did not need the help when I heard the door open again.

"Bartender this guy is a detective, and he has some questions for you!" Michael yelled.

I glared at him as I waited for my ears to stop ringing. I did not want another excitable extrovert around.

There had to be a way to ditch this guy.

"Let me see a badge." The bartender said as he walked to me.

"Here you go." I told him as I pulled out my wallet and showed him my private detective badge. "I'm looking for a guy named Geoffrey Keller. I am aware that he usually spends his time here."

"Lots of people come and go. I can't be expected to remember everyone." The bartender said shaking his head.

The man had been trained well.

"He's asking for a bribe." Michael fake whispered.

"No. I mean I see a lot of people coming and going." The bartender said. "Do you have a picture?"

"Yes. I do." I said putting my hand in my wallet and conjured a folded picture of the guy in my hand which I gave to him.

The bartender unfolded it and took a good look at the picture. "What did he do?"

"He missed his child support payment." I lied.

"I've seen this guy before." The bartender said and then he pointed upward. "He usually sits over there."

"Thanks." I said as I turned to look at the specific area where he was pointing. Guests sat around in booths chatting and drinking with their friends.

The owner considers him an important customer." The bartender said. "I would be careful if I were you."

"I know what I am dealing with." I said as I turned back to him.

"I got your back buddy. No matter how dangerous this guy is." Michael said giving me a double thumbs up.

I planned on getting Marcus to hypnotize him to leave me alone.

"Now that we are past that I would like a club soda." I said, tapping the table.

Terrible tasting drink but now that I knew the section where Geoffrey is going to sit all I had to do is wait and kill time.

CHAPTER 19

"The guy your chasing has arrived." The bartender said.

"Thanks." I said placing the money on the table and turning around,

Now that I knew he was here it was time to contact Marcus. It would be easier for him to come to me than it would be for me to walk into the mass of jumping bodies on the dance floor.

'I have found him.' I texted Marcus.

When ten minutes passed and I failed to receive a response, I stood up. I knew that I would have to go and find him.

I was at the time very optimistic because so far nothing bad had happened since we entered the club. I know they say don't count your chickens before they hatch but I was feeling really good about this.

Which was a clear sign that I had learnt nothing.

"Are we going to confront him?" Michael asked as he took a gulp of his scotch.

"Sorry buddy." I said shaking my head. "You lack the necessary hundred hours to work on a case. It would be irresponsible to bring you with me."

Of course, he did not let it go that easily.

"Can't you deputize me?" Michael asked.

This guy was the type that made me want to slam his head on the bar table and I knew I would not feel an ounce of guilt about it.

"I could use your help." I said, giving him a nod. "You should stay here and keep an eye out if he tries to run through the front door."

"You can count on me." Michael said leaning on to the bar.

I just held back the desire to shake my head and then walked away.

Finding Marcus was not hard. He wasn't one for subtlety so all I had to do was search for the area with the most people and there he would be. I had to push through people dancing on the floor and I will admit I enjoyed doing so because if I had to be uncomfortable and had to go out of my way so should they.

I found Marcus dancing with a girl that had black hair with red highlights as it met her back and went down her back. Her skin tone was the color of a healthy peach, and she had storm grey eyes and he looked to be enjoying himself.

"Marcus I found Geoffry. He's here. It's time to move." I said feeling very happy when I interrupted them and saw the irritation in his eyes.

"Sarah, can you give us a moment?" Marcus asked her as he held her hand.

"Just a moment." Sarah said with a nod and moved back a bit.

"Seriously? Can it not wait a moment?" Marcus asked. "Has Ethan contacted you and told you that Bryan has arrived?"

"Not yet but we can't risk wasting the chance that we have." I said. "You were supposed to start the introductions. We have no idea how long Geoffrey might be staying here or how far away Bryan is."

"I understand." Marcus said frowning. "Give me a minute and I will be right there."

"One minute." I agreed while gritting my teeth. "I am going to head up there first."

Arguing with Marcus would just end up wasting more time than I currently might have.

"Thanks." Marcus said giving me two thumbs up then he walked over to black-haired woman talking with her friends.

One had beach-like blonde hair and the other had orangish- red hair that reached to her shoulders.

As I walked to the stairs that led to the second floor, I was so tempted to burn this place to the ground.

Geoffrey sat at his table on his phone looking at text messages without a worry. He was sitting at the booth with a woman that had curly brown hair and chocolate brown eyes. She was wearing a blue Jacket over a red shirt and a black skirt.

I would soon learn her name is Stephanie.

I noticed the champagne bottle between the two of them a bit reluctant of ruining their night. I had no idea the type of person Geoffrey could be. Stephanie could be perfectly aware of what Geoffrey is.

Vampires for all they had been trusted with helping keep the secret of magic were also the ones that put the secret at risk the most.

His head snapped up and looked at me. I assume he heard me approaching with his enhanced hearing.

"Geoffrey Keller." I said as I walked to the table.

"Yes?" he asked with a curious tone as he put his phone away and his green eyes searched me up and down. "Can I help you?"

It felt like he was assessing whether I was a possible threat to him. Either that or as a possible additional snack that he could drain.

Fighting in this location would be very difficult. There were too many people around that could be turned into weapons against me, little to no room to maneuver around, plenty of objects that could be broken down into sharp edges and tossed at me.

"I am Alex Blackwell a private detective." I told him as I stood in front of the table and put my hands up. "I don't mean to start trouble. In fact, I have some information for you that I think you might want to hear."

"Really now?" Geoffrey asked. "What kind of information and am I going to like it?"

"I would prefer if we could talk privately." I said glancing at the other person at the table.

"You can say anything that you want in front of her." Geoffrey said as he put his shoulder around his companion. "I can make her forget anything that is said."

He had the typical arrogance found in a Vampire. The arrogance that came from living past a normal lifespan, of seeing ages begin and end, and of ending lives that would have lived had they not run into him.

"That is not happening." I said as I glared at him. "What you are hinting at is enough for me to arrest you."

"You certainly have a flair for the dramatic." Geoffrey said with a sigh but turned to his companion. "Stephanie darling, I hate to ruin our night, but can you give the detective what he wants? You do not have to go too far."

"Sure. No problem." Stephanie said as she finished her drink then stood up and walked away from the table.

"Alright." Geoffrey said gesturing to the booth with a smile. "Now that we are alone what kind of information are you bringing me and what do you want for it?"

I looked to the sides before conjuring a chair and taking a seat.

"I came here to warn you that you are being stalked." I said looking in his eyes. "There is a wizard that plans on sacrificing you in a ritual."

"That sounds horrible. Tell me more." Geoffrey said lifting his glass and taking a drink. "Do you know what I have done to anger this man?"

"I can give you an abridged version later. Right now, we should move in case he arrives. I have a safe place we can keep you until this is over." I said as I stood up and walked to the railing.

I glanced at the front door. This is the part of the story where Bryan would arrive, and we would lose Geoffrey amidst the chaos.

"Okay let's go." Geoffrey said pulling out his phone. "I'll text Stephanie that I will call her later."

When did this mystery adventure become a telenovela? These vampires and their love lives were messing up my plans.

"Let's go through the backdoor to the alley." I said as I led the way to the stairs.

I found Marcus leaning against the stairs waiting for us.

"That was five minutes." I said lifting my fingers. "What happened?"

"I planned on keeping our conversation short. She wanted to give me her number and promise that I would call." Marcus defended. "Afterwards I heard you talking to Geoffrey, and it seemed that things were going well so I let you handle it."

"Did you hypnotize her to do that?" I asked him as we neared the steps.

"No, I didn't." Marcus denied with outraged offence. "The only reason I did it to the detective earlier was because I know you wouldn't have asked without a little help."

"What do you think our chances are that this ends well?" Marcus asked me as we watched Geoffrey leave his booth.

"Hopefully very high." I answered.

"Who are you?" Geoffrey asked as he looked at Marcus while walking down the stairs.

I was just happy to be leaving this club earlier than expected so I wasn't going to overthink things and become super paranoid.

That optimism is what got us in this mess. If I had been more suspicious maybe none of what happened next would have had to happen.

CHAPTER 20

"Where do you plan on taking me?" Geoffrey asked as we walked to the nightclub's back door.

"My team and I have come up with a secure location to discuss our next moves." I said as I pushed on the door handle with my left hand and pulled out my phone with my right. "I am texting our associate that we have found you and that he should drive to the rendezvous point."

The wind sent a chill down my spine as I stepped outside of the club and held the door open. According to the information from Marcus and Ethan's earlier trip the door locked from the inside.

I wanted to make sure that the door stayed open so I could keep track of Geoffrey.

"I am wondering what your team gets out of warning me?" Geoffrey asked.

"I want to stop Bryan because I detest his actions." I answered. "Every day he lives free he brings darkness. With each life he takes from his victims for his purposes he creates more with the suffering of their surviving friends and families. I may not be able to bring them all peace, but I can prevent more victims from being made."

"Looks like we have a problem." Marcus said as he walked into the alley.

"What?" I asked him as I looked at him. "Is something happening in the club?"

"The problem is not in the club. Look down the alley." Marcus answered looking in the direction. "The bouncer that we placed against the wall is gone."

"What?" I asked as I moved from the door to see what he was talking about.

It turns out that he was right. In the time that we had been in the club it seems that the bouncer had managed to wake up.

"Where do you think that he is?" I asked, looking at the edge of the alley and wondering if he was searching inside the club for us right now.

"Unless you want to get crushed you might want to move." Geoffrey said.

I jumped forward to gain distance before I looked to see the bouncer slamming into the ground where I had been standing with his fist in a downward punch that cracked the asphalt.

Great it seems that this guy is the type to hold a grudge.

"Come on man." Marcus said. "Like Philadelphia needed more potholes."

"You snapped my neck, robbed me, and left me in a piss- soaked alley." The bouncer growled. "I hope you find it as funny when I pluck your eyes out and feed them to you."

"Can't you let bygones be bygones?" I asked as I conjured an axe behind my back. "I gave you back your sunglasses."

"You think so? You believe that I should just let it go?" The bouncer asked with his red eyes glaring at me.

"Would you be surprised if I said yes?" I asked as I pointed the axe at him. "Now you can let us go on our way or we make this a fight that you will regret picking."

The bouncer never got to answer my ultimatum as Geoffrey ran behind him and slammed him headfirst against the club wall so hard that it caused a spiderweb-like indentation to form.

"You are too soft wizard." Geoffrey said slamming the bouncer's head against the brick wall again. "When someone comes to challenge you, the only choice is to make sure they can never do it again."

"Who are you?" The bouncer asked groaning as he stumbled towards Geoffrey. "The last thing that you will ever see." Geoffrey said with a laugh.

The next second he plunged his hand into the bouncer's chest. I did not see it happening, but I could hear the gasp the bouncer made before he fell to the ground and his skin started to turn grey.

Depending on the vampire's age when killed it will either become dust or become a grey corpse. The corpse being left behind means that they were younger than two centuries.

"Seriously?" I asked looking at him and his bloody hand before I kneeled next to the dead body that I would now have to take care of.

"He picked this fight. He should have prepared for it to end badly for him." Geoffrey said as he looked at the heart in his hand and the blood on his fingers. "That is a lesson the two of you are going to learn soon enough."

What?

"Turn around!" Marcus shouted.

I turned to see Stephanie standing at the entrance of the alley holding a gun aimed at me.

"What is going on here Geoffrey?" I asked as I took a step to the side to try and move from the direction the gun was pointing.

She kept the gun aimed at me every step of the way.

I didn't know much about guns besides that they hurt when you were hit with them, and the country had a real problem with managing those that they allowed to buy them. If I lived past this situation, I would be a much stronger supporter for gun control. I would have tried teleporting but that wasn't safe given my lack of focus and with Geoffrey's speed the moment I reappeared he would snap my neck faster than I could blink.

I glanced towards him "Why are you making her do this?"

"Do you need to know?" Geoffrey asked. "Will the mystery keep your soul bound to this world until you get an answer?"

I could hear the cheer in his voice as he taunted me.

"I am really getting tired of guns." Marcus growled from behind me. "Too many of them have been pointed at us this week."

"We came here to save your life, and this is how you repay us?" I asked.

"Do it Stephanie." Geoffrey said ignoring me.

The moment that he finished his sentence she pulled the trigger and bullets came flying at me. The next sound I heard was the whoosh that accompanied vampires when they ran and found Marcus standing in front of me.

Situations like this are why I ignore all the headaches that dealing with him brings.

"You are going to regret that." Marcus said as he crouched to the ground.

The moment he healed he charged at Stephanie. He was there one moment then all I heard was the crack of a neck and when he reappeared, he was behind Stephanie and then I just saw her falling down to the ground.

I swiftly turned back to Geoffrey to see the expression on his face. I wondered how he would react to this. Would he be snarling in anger or crying at his loss? Depending on the response it would change how we fought this guy.

The first thing that I noticed was that Geoffrey looked genuinely happy at Stephanie's body lying on the ground. He had a grin on his face that seemed like we had just solved all of his problems for him.

I thought that was a rather cruel way to break up with someone.

Jokes aside clearly, he was up to something. However, while he was distracted thinking of whatever demented scheme he had going I conjured a wooden javelin in the air and tried to move it into his heart with telekinesis.

Unfortunately, he grabbed it right when it entered his range, and his strength prevented it from moving further.

"I have to admit that this is nice workmanship." Geoffrey said, closing his fingers around it and then spun the javelin in a circle between his hands. "I am going to borrow this for a moment."

The next blink of an eye and he was gone.

Hearing a gasp of pain, I turned behind me and saw the javelin stabbing through Marcus's heart. As his body slumped down to the ground, I saw it turning grey and his veins became more obvious.

Now it was just me and a psychotic vampire alone in an alley. I had no wand nor my coat full of enchanted items, but he had all his strength and speed and was completely unpredictable. The odds weren't in my favor of coming out ahead in this.

This location was horrible. I needed to get some distance so that I did not worry about the possible enemy behind my back.

I glanced at the direction that I wanted to move. The next moment he pushed me to the ground.

"Before you think of running remember that I can run to either end of the alley before you even make your first step." Geoffrey said.

"You looked happy when she died so why are you doing this?" I questioned him.

None of his actions made sense. He was trying to kill people that were here to save his life. He had avenged his girlfriend though he is the one that put her at risk and the reason she died.

"I did not kill your friend because he killed Stephanie. I had fed her my blood hours ago. In fact, I had been wondering how to kill her for a while without her coming back and hating me and your friend provided the solution. I treat all annoyances the same." Geoffrey taunted. "Anyway, she will rise up again in a few hours."

This was not good news. That meant I would be outnumbered and could be dealing with an old vampire and a starving transitioning human. I had to beat him before the girl woke up or I was going to lose this fight. It was hours away from sunrise so even time was against me.

"That just means that I would have to fight even harder and kill you before she wakes up." I said as I conjured a small hatchet and came at him with a swing to his neck.

I refused to be killed in an alley after all I hadn't gotten Ethan his vengeance or gotten paid and that was all the motivation I needed.

"Yes! This is what I wanted. I love it when prey fights back." Geoffrey said excitedly as he backed up and took a boxing stance looking excited over what was going to happen. "Bryan said I should lead you into a trap, but this is feels better."

"You are working with the man that wants to sacrifice you?" I asked as I tried to slice the axe into his shoulder with a downward swing. "What is wrong with you?"

He twisted to the side and countered with a right punch that sent me stumbling to the wall.

That punch hurt. The next three punches to the stomach happened in quick succession and caused me to drop the axe to the floor. It was likely that after this fight I was going to have bruises and those bruises would have bruises.

However, at the moment there was no time to focus on the future. First, I would need to win this fight.

"You are the detective." Geoffrey said backing up again so that I could get some freedom. "Why don't you solve the mystery?"

It was like we were in elementary school, and he was the big bad bully. Except when he was done playing, I would be dead.

CHAPTER 21

There is a grim smile on my face as I looked up at the vampire that is threatening my life. The vampire that I had come here to try and help. I remembered those little moments where I chose to keep fighting and searching for the truth.

It turns out that I had walked through the labyrinth only to find the end of the maze held a deep and dark pit.

To make matters worse Geoffrey picked up the hatchet that I had dropped, and he took a few practice swings.

I glared at him. If I was going to fight for my life, then I would do it with weapons that I preferred.

I conjured two short swords. The sword held in the left hand is black and the other sword held in the right is white. There is a yin-yang symbol on the base with the white and black stretching up the blades with their inverse colors. They were based on the swords Kanshou and Byakuya of type-moon which was based upon the story of Gan Jiang and Mo Ye.

"What type of swords are those?" Geoffrey asked, looking at them.

"The best type. These are the swords that I use when I really want to stab through a bastard." I said charging at him.

Strengthening magic worked through the process of sending mana through the desired limbs. The process reinforced the legs so that you could run hundreds of laps as long as you had mana.

Even though I wasn't exactly a fan of running long distances I enchanted my sneakers to make sure that they would survive the process in case such a situation was needed.

It did not make me as fast as a vampire, but it would raise my chances.

With the angle it looked like I planned to slice alongside his shoulder with my left and he raised the hatchet to try and defend as I knew he would. Vampires could heal their injuries better than when they were alive but not enough to heal a severed limb.

As he was too busy with dodging the black sword in my left hand, he did not notice that that I planned to stab him in the stomach with the white sword in my right.

I quickly jumped backwards landing next to Marcus's body.

"You finally made contact." Geoffrey said with a smile on his face as he looked at the sword stabbing him. "I guess that is my turn now."

"This is not a game of tag you demented psycho." I said using telekinesis to rip the sword back to me. I felt joy as he fell to the ground in pain.

While he was healing I apported the hatchet back to my office. I did not need Bryan having a tool he could use to search for me.

Now that I had gotten what I needed it was time to go. I put my hand on his chest and teleported us to the rendezvous point.

I just shook my head and walked to the nearest pillar and took a seat glaring at the ground. Fifteen minutes later my car arrived and parked in the space across from us.

"What happened?" Ethan asked after he walked out of the car and looked down at Marcus.

"We were blindsided. That is what happened." I said punching my fist against the ground. "This whole night has turned into an incredible disaster."

"What does that mean?" Ethan asked concerned. "Did Bryan show up after I left? Did he take Geoffrey?"

"I wouldn't be as angry if that is what happened." I said glaring at the ground. "It seems that Bryan and Geoffrey are working together."

"How much do they know?" Ethan asked shocked and turning his head to the parking garage entrance. "Is he aware of the rendezvous point? Your office? Do you think we are going to have to fight our way out of here?"

"He should not know where we are" I said shaking my head. "I only told him that we had a secure location to take him."

"What are we going to do now?" Ethan asked as he started pacing. "We have to hurry otherwise before Bryan performs his ritual and becomes immortal."

"I already thought of that and have a way to track them." I said as I stood up and opened the trunk.

I placed the sword inside.

"Before that though we have to deal with this." I said gesturing to Marcus's body.

"Whatever plan you have I hope that it happens quickly." Ethan said. "We have to avenge both Marcus's and my death."

"Marcus will certainly appreciate your desire." I said as I lifted the javelin from his chest.

"How can you still make jokes?" Ethan asked. "Your partner has died?"

"He was already dead when I met him and just like before he will wake up again." I said with a smile. "Now is the hard part."

"What?" Ethan asked.

"We drive back to the office." I said using telekinesis to lift him back to the car.

"How is that the hard part?" Ethan asked.

"My seats are going to be smeared with his blood." I said walking to the trunk and placing the swords inside. "Even after I clean the seats, I am going to remember that. It hurts me emotionally."

I needed them for my plan, so I wanted to make sure that they were safe in my workshop. After I slammed the trunk shut, I went back to the driver's seat. "Get in."

"He looks like his skin is regaining color." Ethan said looking back at Marcus's body.

"Great." I said taking a left turn. "He should wake up in four hours."

"How do you know that?" Ethan asked. "Test had been conducted."

When a vampire was knocked unconscious by something like a snapped neck the time it took for them to heal and regain consciousness depended on their age. For young vampires it took four hours for them to awaken. Each century reduced that time by twenty minutes.

"So, the whole staking vampires through the heart to kill them is a lie?" Ethan asked.

"No that is true." I answered. "However, I would be a pretty terrible enchanter if I let that stop me. The ring that Marcus wears is an item I enchanted. I had based it off of the enchantment of the gem of Amara on Buffy."

It would allow him to survive all the common vampire weaknesses. It was another reason I was fond of books and television. People in this world have spent so long coming up with ideas for enchanted items it would be a waste to not use them as inspiration in my business.

"Really?" Ethan asked glancing at the ring.

"Yes. Unless his head is cut off, his heart extracted, or his ring hand taken off and then staked, Marcus is likely to survive. "I answered.

It didn't stop him from sleeping in late though.

"So, you work as a psychic detective and on the side sell magical items?" Ethan asked.

"The need for magical items is very in demand and there was always someone looking for one of them. So even if I have a month with low level cases I have a backup income."

"So, what type of enchantments do you sell?" Ethan asked.

"My major enchantments act as protection charms, create barriers, and grant good luck." I said as I took a right turn so I could park in front of my office.

Unfortunately, others were not as cautioned and concerned as I when it came to selling enchanted items.

"You need to help me bring him in." I said, looking at my office as I parked the car.

"What is the matter?" Ethan asked.

"My door is open." I said with a frown. "The door had been locked when we had left."

"I thought you had not told Geoffrey about the office?" Ethan asked.

"I didn't." I confirmed. "However, there are plenty of ways to gather information with magic without the other party being aware."

"How do you want to handle this?" Ethan asked.

"You can go in first." I said as I placed Marcus against the floor of the car. "Turn invisible and take a look around. If you feel that there is something suspicious going on inside, I want you to phase through the roof and signal me with a text from the phone I gave you."

"Alright." Ethan said before he disappeared.

I teleported behind the car using it as a shield and the darkness for cover. The seconds passed as I glanced to the side waiting for something to explode. My eyes snapped to my phone as it began to vibrate.

"Yes." I answered looking at my office with suspicious eyes.

"There is no one here but I did find something strange." Ethan said.

"What is it?" I asked as I started rising to my feet.

"I have no idea." Ethan said. "It is on your business table."

I sprinted to the wall next to my office and glanced inside. I looked at the table that I used for meetings and saw what Ethan had been looking at.

The object was a circular ball the size of a bell chime.

I walked into the office with a frown and picked up the object with a sigh. "Just great."

"Do you know what it is?" Ethan asked.

"That is a shamanavash." I said with my fingers clenching around it. "It is how people beyond the Alter-plane send messages. Both pre-recorded and in actual time."

"Do you think Bryan left it here as a way to taunt us?" Ethan asked.

"I would prefer to think that it was a rude deliveryman in a rush but given how disastrous this night has been Bryan leaving it seems to be more likely." I said with a sigh as I rolled the shamanavash in my hand. "We can listen to it in the workshop. Come and help me grab Marcus."

We dragged him into the workshop by his arms and legs.

"What is going on?" Marcus asked announcing he was awake "I refuse to be your sacrifice to whatever volcano god you worship!".

"Shut up." I said in annoyance dropping him as he started moving swiftly left and right.

"What happened Alex?" Marcus asked as he stood back up. "Where is Geoffrey?"

"We had to leave Geoffrey behind." I said as I started explaining what happened after he got stabbed with the javelin.

"When I get my hands on him, he is going to wish that Bryan had killed him." Marcus swore, clenching his fingers into fists.

He was clearly serious about this too. For him this was now about revenge, and he would accept nothing less. As vampires experienced feelings more powerfully than any human it was easy for anger to turn into a desire for vengeance and dislike to turn into an intense hate.

Marcus was a handful when he was playful but when he was in vengeance mode, he could be downright cruel.

"We will but first we need to find out where they are." I said walking down the stairs while I looked at the shamanavash floating beside me.

"How are we going to do that?" Marcus asked.

"I managed to get some of Geoffrey's blood on a sword of mine before I rescued you. We can use that to scry for him." I said as we left the stairs and entered the vast space of my workshop.

I walked to the bench I placed it on and scraped the dried flakes of blood into a vial. Then I replaced the crystal I used for scrying with the vial. I moved to the table that had a map of the city.

"Invenimus." I chanted as I focused on the connection between Geoffrey and his blood.

"Are you sure that this is working?" Marcus asked. "It feels like an hour has passed and you have yet to gain a result."

"Shut up. Bryan must have cloaked Geoffrey somehow." I said, pulling back from the table. "We can find him. It will just take some time."

"Maybe you should check the shamanavash?" Ethan suggested. "Despite whatever taunt or threat, it might hold there is a chance we could use it to find a clue."

"Very well then." I said leaving the scrying table to get some space and pressed the symbol at the center and tossed the shamanavash so it gained some distance. "Let's see what Bryan wants to say."

A large projection of a mask appeared above the shamanavash.

The mask is white, shaped like a dog or a wolf. On the mask were three uneven red scratch marks going through the right eye. The one in the middle was the largest, the one on the right was the shortest, and the last one on the left was in between those two. One the left side there were two red curves going upwards. The eyes, nose, and mouth is a combination of red paint surrounding black paint.

"Hello. If you are hearing this then you have activated the shamanavash and want to hear my message." The masked face said.

He stopped talking and I realized he wanted us to say something back.

"What do you want Bryan?" I asked. "Have you contacted us to mock us over our confrontation with your accomplice?"

"Ask him what is with the weird mask." Marcus said from behind me. "Has his face been deformed by the evil magics he has used?"

I ignored him for the moment and let him perform his role. I did want to see how he would react to the insults though.

"I am not Bryan though I do know him." The masked man denied.

"You are his teacher." I said with realization.

"Who are you?" Ethan asked.

"If I wanted you to know who I am would I be wearing the mask?" The masked man asked. "Rather paradoxical, isn't it? Who is but the form following the function of what and what I am is a man in a mask."

"Is he serious?" Marcus asked.

"Stop it. I am in no mood to listen to the entire speech at the moment." I said annoyed at his reference. "I repeat what do you want?"

"I thought that you would enjoy the joke. You did claim that you were the one that made references" The masked man said. "You may call me Spektral and what I want is to tell you that you still have time. The ritual that Bryan intends to perform will happen tomorrow night when the moon reaches its apex. He has had to move locations because of a certain group finding his hidden warehouse. Geoffrey is currently staying in a cabin protected by a barrier in Lancaster County. It is keeping them hidden by misdirecting anyone that is searches for them."

"I told you." I said as I glanced back at Marcus.

"Do not worry it will fall a few hours before dusk." Spektral said. "Here is the location."

I apported a notepad and pen and started copying the address.

"Why are you telling us this?" Ethan asked with a suspicious tone. "Isn't he your student?"

"Think of your adventure so far as a story." Spektral said. "I have been watching as you detectives have chased after Bryan. Seeing the horror that you felt when you found the bodies, the defiance you displayed as you overcame challenges, the hope that grew as you found clues, and the anguish you experienced as you realized that you were fooled."

"You want to see how this story ends?" I asked as my eye began to twitch.

"I noticed that as I walked through your office that you are a fan of stories." Spektral said. "Don't you just hate it when you find a story that holds your interest only for the author to suddenly stop without giving a proper ending?"

"You are as insane as your student!" Ethan shouted. "Do you know how many people have died because of what you taught him?"

"If you want to stop him then all you have to do is catch him." Spektral said in an uncaring tone. "I am just calling so that you lot stay motivated, and I see that I have. My work is done."

He ended the call and the red color of the shamanavash turned dim.

"Are you going to go after him as well?" Ethan asked.

"I will start searching for him after we take Bryan down." I said, putting my arm on his shoulder. "I have a friend with the ability of psychometry. She can search the history of the Shamanavash and give me a lead on how to find him."

CHAPTER 22

"I have put the address in." I said as I walked to my desk and pulled my trench coat off from the chair.

"So, we are going to be fighting an evil wizard in a dark and creepy forest?" Ethan asked. "Does anyone else feel uncomfortable about this?"

"Yes, but this is our final chance to stop Bryan." I said as my trench coat turned into a tan brown.

"Why do you think that he chose those woods?" Marcus said as he placed his arms behind his back and began leaning on the window. "Has he never heard of Hansel and Gretel?"

"I seriously hate that story." I grumbled as I walked to the door and opened it.

"You are just saying that because it was based on a true story." Marcus said bouncing forward.

"No, it wasn't. They decided to make an insane cannibal into a witch to help sell a story." I refuted as we walked to the car. "Anyway, we don't have time for this."

"Driving there is going to take at least two hours. That means we will have plenty of time to talk." Marcus challenged.

"Marcus." Ethan called out.

"Yes?" Marcus responded.

"If everything happens as we expect I will be sent to the great beyond, so I have something to ask while I have the time." Ethan said.

"What is it?" Marcus asked.

"Why do vampires say they eat people when they drink their blood?" Ethan asked.

"I don't know, maybe because it sounds better than saying you have to suck people to live." He said with a grin on his face which Ethan caught on to and started laughing.

I just sighed at the idiots that I had been stuck with. "Instead, they prefer for people to think that they are cannibals and eat humans as if they were a steak. Possibly with a side of fava beans and a nice chianti."

"I know a couple of vampires that do that." Marcus admitted. "I never really got the appeal."

"So, what type of people do you pick when you get hungry?" Ethan asked.

"I don't eat people." Marcus said.

"Then you eat survive on the blood of animals?" Ethan asked him.

"It is possible to survive on animal blood, but I prefer to drink human blood." Marcus said.

"Then how do you survive if you don't eat people?" Ethan asked him.

"I have people who "donate" me blood." Marcus said.

"He prefers to let his food come to him. He has groups of people purely hypnotized just for the purpose of putting their blood in bags and bringing them to him. I believe he has different people for every day of the week." I clarified.

"I need some variety otherwise I might get bored." Marcus defended.

"Wow, I don't know if that is pure genius or just lazy." Ethan said.

"For Marcus it was both." I said while taking a turn.

"At least with my system they are not at risk of being drained dry." Marcus said. "I think that you two should be amazed at my control and care for sapient life."

"Why do you go through all of that work?" Ethan asked. "Is it because of the magic council?"

"Killing people for blood only makes vampire hunters and I am not going to spend my immortal life running from someone who wants revenge on me." Marcus answered. "Like how right now we are hunting for Bryan because of the way that he chose his victims."

Marcus had told me that situation is one of the major fears that he had about his immortal life. The chance that someone might become a vampire hunter and track him down for revenge for someone that he had drained.

It is why he focused so much on his hypnotism.

"How close are we?" Ethan asked.

"If we keep going at this pace that we would arrive at the location in about twenty minutes." I told him as I looked at the g.p.s.'s estimation of our arrival.

"We might get there too early." Marcus said. "The sun is just starting to go down."

He was not wrong. Currently the sky is a warm orange as the sun started its descent.

"We should use the time to prepare and come up with a plan."

This was one of the best times for them to do it. If we talk about it during the trek to Bryan's cabin, we might risk having Geoffrey overhear us.

"I would ask if you were ready for this fight but that would probably be a stupid question, right?" Ethan asked.

"How do we start?" Marcus asked, at the place where Bryan intended to conduct his ritual.

"I plan on using the vial to lead us to Geoffrey. I assume he will be guarding the cabin while Bryan prepares what he needs for the ritual." I said as I started imagining what would happen when we showed up and tried to stop Bryan's ritual to become immortal. "I want you two to surround the cabin from different sides. I will gain Geoffrey's attention by threatening to have Marcus burn the cabin down to the ground."

"Not too difficult." Marcus said.

"While I have his attention Ethan will phase through the cabin behind Geoffrey with a stake to stab him through his heart." I continued.

"How will we find Bryan then?" Marcus asked. "If we kill our only lead then we may never find him. He just escapes and tries with another vampire."

"I doubt he will tell us where to find his partner. After we stake Geoffrey, I will use something at the cabin that Bryan touched to lead us to him." I answered him as I turned off of the highway. "After we take down Geoffrey we search for Bryan. Ethan will take to the skies and Marcus you will listen for any movement. Ethan will gain his attention then you and I will strike before he has the time to say a single word."

"Are you sure that this is the right place?" Marcus asked as he looked out of the car window.

"According to the g.p.s. the place that we are looking for is straight ahead." I said looking at the woods as I parked in a nearby parking lot. "Marcus do you hear anything?"

"I can hear the sound of squirrels running across the ground, birds flapping their wings as they return to their nests and the fish swimming through the rushing Conestoga River." Marcus answered. "But if you are asking if I can hear our targets talking? Then I am sorry to say that no. I do not hear any people besides us. We may be too far out of range."

"Could it have been a trick?" Ethan asked annoyed. "A way for Spektral to waste our time and let his student finish his plans?"

"It could be possible but do not worry." I said as I left the car, looked at the surroundings and pulled out my sunglasses. "I have another way for us to check."

When I put my sunglasses on, I saw the barrier that covered the land. The woods looked creepy enough to me already but looking at that dome I believed that feeling was going to multiply.

The dome is a black deeper than any I had seen before. I believed that if someone made a maze in that darkness anyone brave enough to try and reach the end would end up walking for their entire lives trying to find their hand in front of their face let alone walk to the other side. A darkness that intruded upon the world and it seemed as if it is trying to reach the sky and swallow the sun above and corrupt its shining light.

Now if Spektral was telling the truth we just had to wait for it to fall.

"We are in the right place. I can see the barrier." I said as I glanced at the ground.

At the edge of the dome are runes that stretched far into the distance and if I were to assume in the shape of a circle that covered the woods. Right now, they glowed with the intensity of an ominous fire. As the minutes passed and the moon rose higher in the sky they would dim and then eventually vanish.

I put my hand in my trench coat pocket and pulled out a bag of candied peach rings.

"One last snack before we face possible death?" Marcus asked.

"Do you want one?" I asked Marcus.

"Sure." Marcus said, as he his hand out and turned to the forest. "Food is a welcome distraction from the mess ahead of us."

"I thought that you would be looking forward to this." Ethan said. "The atmosphere seems perfect for the fight that is about to go down."

"You would be wrong." Marcus said. "I checked before we left, Tonight is a waxing gibbous not a full moon, just like his house this night is a disappointment."

I ignored his complaining as I was just hoping that I could make it back out of those woods in one piece.

"In times like this the main character would give a big grand speech to motivate us." I said looking at the woods. "I haven't prepared anything like that, but I feel that this works. We may be vastly different people joined together for varied reasons, but we are here to avenge those lives that have been tragically cut short. So as long as we work together, they cannot stand against us."

"I am already all in." Ethan said. "He has taken too much from way too many people."

"In brightest day or in darkest night let's give this bastard a fright." Marcus said.

I watched as the moon rose higher in the sky and the runes with their diminished glow started vanishing. It happened like knocked over dominos. One rune vanished then the next followed quickly. The black dome surrounding the woods began to pulsate and recede inwards.

"The barrier has fallen." I said putting the candies back in my trench coat and pulling out my scrying rope that is connected to the vial of Geoffrey's blood. "Now nothing is protecting them from my scrying."

If Bryan has no idea that this is happening, then this is probably the result of some enchanted item he was given. Which just made all of this more confusing. Spektral claimed that all this was for entertainment, but this was not the type of effort that someone would go through just to have a couple of laughs.

There was a purpose behind all of this, and I would need to figure it out.

"Can you make a light?" Marcus asked. "We do not need you tripping on a stone and breaking your leg."

Casting two spells at the same time is not an easy feat. It required training to split your focus and stay aware of how much mana you were spending.

"Magnum lumen." I said and three balls of light appeared around me illuminating the park in glowing blue light.

I could change the colors if I wished but these were the best for the situation. We walked into the woods with determined eyes.

The further we walked into the woods the more it felt like we were in an isolated world even without the dome. The long branches of the trees reached to the sky blocking the sight of the parking lot.

"Why do you think that he chose this place to set up a hideout?" Marcus asked.

"There are plenty of possible reasons. It could be because it gives him cover to hide and plenty of trees to practice his spells on." I answered before taking a turn west and then we came to a fork in the road.

The vial floated to the left.

"This way." I said turning to follow the path.

We continued walking straight for ten minutes then walked up a hill.

"Wait." Marcus suddenly said, running to the front of the group.

"What's going on?" I asked, turning to him.

"I can hear Geoffrey." Marcus said as he crouched on the ground and closed his eyes. "He is talking to Bryan."

If he could hear them speaking, then that must have meant that we were close to whatever cabin they were staying in.

"Bryan is at the cabin?" I asked crouching as well. "What are they saying?"

Depending on the situation the plan might have to be changed. Maybe it was for the best that we did not say a word and just burned the place to the ground?

"I do not think Bryan is there. I think that they are talking on the phone." Marcus answered. "I can hear Geoffrey voice clearly, but Bryan's is a little more difficult."

"What can you hear?" I asked.

"He is telling Geoffrey to go and bring Stephanie to the ritual circle. That it is time to carve the sigils on her. Afterwards he is to head to the basement. Apparently, Bryan cast some sort of protection spell on the area." Marcus answered.

"That is not good." I said frowning.

Going by what protections he has already we needed to make sure that he did not enter it.

"Stephanie is awake?" Ethan asked. "Has she completed the transition?"

"Seems like it." Marcus answered.

"How?" Ethan asked. "I thought she needed to drink human blood?"

"Bryan probably gave her some of his to complete the process." I said as I stood up. "Do you think it would be too much to ask the universe that it has left him so weak he can barely walk?"

"Do you think the universe will listen?" Marcus asked following after me.

"No but I would like to believe." I said as I turned to look over the hill and into the distance. "Now that we are in range try to be as quiet as possible."

"We are going to ruin this night for Bryan faster than an overprotective dad on prom night." Marcus said.

I truly must have done something truly horrible to someone in a past life.

Taking a right turn I led the group and then we walked down the rocky path that led back to the ground.

After five more minutes of walking straight we found the cabin. It stood in a clearing that was a little past the river and surrounded by trees.

I pointed at the sides of the cabin and watched as Marcus and Ethan went to take their positions behind the trees. Then I let the light spell vanish, counted to three in my head, and walked towards the cabin.

"Vehementi Impetu." I said with my wand aimed the at cabin and watched as the blast of energy traveled and smashed into the door.

The door held together for the most part, but cracks were starting to appear at the edges. I was not discouraged. Despite how magically reinforced the door seemed to be breaking inside was not my goal.

What I wanted is to get the attention of the vampire residing inside.

So, I cast the spell five more times. Hammering away at the brown door watching as more and more of the door began to chip as it slammed against the frame.

"Are you coming out or do I have to act like the big bad wolf and blow this house down?" I shouted.

Just as I was about to blast the door again, I noticed the doorknob was turning.

I was tempted to say the words again just to see if it would cause it to fly into his face and knock him flat on his back.

"If you wanted an invitation to come inside all you had to do was ask." Geoffrey said standing on the other side of the door with a smile on his face. "Your friend on the other hand is going to have a problem entering. So sad but at least he will have the comfort of hearing you in your final moments."

"That is not much of a problem since you are going to be coming outside." I said grateful that I was not close enough to have to hear another innuendo from Marcus.

"Why would I do that?" Geoffrey asked as he tilted his head. "There are so many wonderfully sharp things inside that I can throw through you. As if I were a caveman trying to spear a fish for dinner."

"Because my vampire friend is going to burn this place to the ground if you don't." I threatened moving closer to the door while waiting for Ethan to get behind him. "I doubt that you want to burn to death."

"Then you would be sacrificing Stephanie." Geoffrey boasted. "Another innocent caught up in a game she does not understand."

"If she is the final sacrifice need to stop you and Bryan, I would be willing to make the call." I lied pulling a coin from my trench coat. "The moment this coin touches the ground is the moment this place goes up in smoke."

"You're bluffing." Geoffrey denied.

"Watch." I said and let the coin fall.

Geoffrey's eyes followed it intent on seeing my threat through.

The coin hit the ground with a sound clear to both vampires. However, despite the seconds passing by there is no sign of a fire.

"Such a shame." Geoffrey taunted. "It seems that your friend is not as cold as you seem to be."

"Well, that is awkward." I said pretending to be annoyed.

My smile had to be suppressed. He was so focused on the coin and on mocking me that he never thought that he might be in actual danger.

Ethan stood behind him ready with the stake and wanting to be sure I used telekinesis to enhance both the speed and strength of the thrust as Ethan stabbed it through him.

"What?" Geoffrey asked, falling through the door and onto my shoulders.

"You tricked me back at Blood Moon." I said, bringing the coin back into my hand. "I figured one good trick deserves another."

"Fine you win." Geoffrey wheezed as his skin started graying. "Though I want you to know that whatever afterlife I end up in I will be cursing you to live an eternity of misery and."

He fell to the ground and then turned to ash.

"I hope your pettiness brings you peace in the underworld." I said with annoyance as I started dusting off the ashes that had fallen onto my clothes.

"That is one down." Marcus said.

I jumped, twisting my head at the vampire standing next to me so fast that I was afraid that I might have hurt my neck.

"How do you feel about how he met his end?" I asked.

"I hoped that he was younger. If I was not going to be the one to kill him then I wanted to torch his bones." Marcus complained with his index finger lit with a dark flame.

All people had a connection to the five elements of nature. Water, Fire, Lightning, Earth, and Air and based on their personalities some elements were stronger in some people than in others. When people transitioned into vampires, they gained the ability to conjure and manipulate those elements.

Lightning made them run faster and improved their already improved reflexes, Earth made them more durable and stronger, Air let them fly, Fire let them burn others, and water drowned their enemies.

The color of the elements however was black. I had the belief it was due to Vampires being created from dark magic.

"All that is left is to save the girl and beat the boss." I said looking at the cabin ahead of us.

"For all the problems Geoffrey caused us he was right about something. How are we going to get me into that cabin?" Marcus asked.

"I thought of that already." I said pulling a glove out of my trench coat. "Here."

"What am I supposed to do with this?" Marcus asked.

"This is the Enchanted Glove: Phantom Thief. This glove will allow you to cheat that rule about invitations." I said.

The downside is that he wouldn't be as strong as he usually was. However, with Geoffrey dead that was not a problem for the moment.

"Cool." Marcus said as he took the glove.

Entering the cabin, I could say that this was more like what I was expecting. While on the outside the cabin looked small and unassuming if you got past the entrance, you could tell that the space had been expanded with magic.

The building is as large as a townhouse. It was as if he had combined two buildings.

Spektral must have been really skilled if he had given him this place.

"Where is Stephanie?" I asked Marcus as I looked around.

"Geoffrey told her to head to the basement." Marcus said as he walked over to the table and looked at the Othello boardgame lying on it. "He probably expected to finish us off quick and come back to get her."

"Ethan." I said, gaining his attention. "Phase through the floor and find out what we might be dealing with."

Ethan returned a few minutes later.

"She is down there." Ethan said with his head rising through the ground. "Be careful though whatever you do don't leave the steps. There are strange symbols all over the walls similar to the ones we had found in the warehouse."

Afterwards he sank back down.

"Alright." I said and walked through the hall and found the doorway to the basement. "Here we go."

As I turned the doorknob, I learned that Stephanie had locked the door when she went through.

"Want me to see if I can rip the door of its hinges?" Marcus asked.

"No. I have another idea." I said and used telekinesis to turn the door latch back to the lock. "Let's go. Remembering the warning."

I gestured to Marcus to lead walk down the steps first. I followed behind him with my wand aimed in front of me ready to cast a spell at a moment's notice and I used the wall to maintain my balance.

Looking around the room I found that sigils had been spray painted in red paint around the room.

"Oh god." Stephanie said, backing away from us in fear. "What did you do to Geoff?"

"What did you say to her?" I asked, turning to Marcus.

"Nothing." Marcus denied. "I did not even get the chance to begin threatening her."

"He has returned to the earth." I said in the nicest way possible.

"You killed him!" Stephanie shrieked, turning from fear to anger as quickly as a ferret chases a chicken.

"Would you feel better if I told you that it was him or us?" Marcus asked.

"You utter bastard!" Stephanie roared as she tried to charge at him.

Then to our surprise we watched as she was tossed backwards as if she had crashed into an invisible wall.

"What?" Marcus asked surprised.

"It might be one of the defenses that Byan talked about." I said looking around. "Do not try to act violently. It might redirect whatever force is used down here against someone else towards themselves."

"Do you sense anything?" Marcus asked.

"All the magic in this cabin is messing with my senses." I said pulling out my glasses.

As I looked at the sigils, I found them lacking any magical energy. However, when I looked at the edge of the stairs, I found a set of black runes. Glowing subtler than the ones that had been outside the dome or the sigils painted around the basement. "I found it. Marcus go and get a bird from outside."

"What?" Marcus asked.

"I said go and capture a bird." I repeated. "I have an idea that I want to test and please do it quick. Time is a huge factor."

"Fine." Marcus said as he vanished.

"This is just like what happened to Marcus at Bryan's house." Ethan remembered.

"I believe that it's a boundary circle. Or well boundary trapezoid in this case." I said frowning in annoyance.

Boundary circles are a type of barrier magic, and they fall under the grand category of warding magic. Wards were created to keep things out that were dangerous and that you considered unfriendly.

Boundary circles are a type of spell that reversed the concept. They are created to keep something trapped inside the area so that it cannot leave.

"What are you talking about?" Stephanie asked, shifting her head. "What are you planning to do to me?"

"What do you understand about what has happened to you?" I asked sitting on the steps.

"I have been turned into a vampire." Stephanie said as she looked at her hands. "Geoff told me that he had a friend who could cure me and turn me back into a human. Until you killed him."

She looked at us with a glare that promised utter vengeance.

Ah. That is how he planned to trick her into walking to her death.

"Sorry but that was a lie." I explained. "You were intended to be a sacrifice by your boyfriend. We are here to save you."

"I don't believe you." Stephanie denied shaking her head. "You are just trying to trick me. Geoff told me that you and your friend were hunting him. Looking to use him to hunt down a friend."

She is in denial. Understandable given her circumstances but not something that I had the time to deal with.

"I found one." Marcus said, surprising us as he reappeared. "I hope that you are happy."

"I am." I said tossing the bird past the steps.

The writing on the ground flashed from purple to red.

"Now for the test." I said using telekinesis to slowly try and bring the bird back to my hand.

The moment the bird tried to pass the steps the runes glowed red and stopped its progress. Satisfied, I let the bird fall back to the ground watching in squawk in confusion.

"So, if someone walked past the steps they would be stuck as well?" Ethan asked. "Why would Bryan tell Geoffrey to head to the basement after he brought Stephanie to the ritual circle?"

His instructions made sense if you considered that this was intended to be a trap.

"I will explain later." I said, reaching into my trench coat and pulling out my laser pointer. "Marcus the moment that I break the spell snap her neck."

"What?" Stephanie asked as she started backing away.

"Do not worry. You will be fine." I said as I aimed the light at the bottom of the steps and watched as with each second the runes began to grow lighter, and the spell began to weaken. "As I told you earlier, we are going to save you."

It took five minutes for the spell to break.

I heard as her neck snapped and she fell unconscious into Marcus's arms.

"Now there is only one person left to deal with." I said, turning to the stairs.

"Do you think that he knows we have ruined his ritual?" Ethan asked.

It was at that moment that Marcus's phone began to play a ringtone.

"It seems that Spektral has sent us a message." Marcus said showing me the phone and tossing it.

"You had to say something." I said to Ethan with a scowl as I caught the phone.

"What is the matter?" Ethan asked.

"The message says "*Congratulations on freeing Stephanie. However, I feel like I should tell you that breaking the runes has activated another trap. That we should leave fast if we want to live.*" It even has a smiley face emoji." I said with a scowl before I felt a chill go down my spine and my blood freeze as I felt a surge of prana.

While I did not trust Spektral I felt that this was good advice. I had no idea what was going on, but I doubted that I wanted to be inside this cabin and find out.

"Hurry." I said before teleporting outside.

I watched as a large circle finished forming around the cabin. Prana moved from the runes around the circle. Flowing through the ground as if it were magma towards the cabin.

"What is happening?" Ethan asked as he floated through the door. "It felt like an earthquake is happening inside the cabin."

"It seems that the house is being dragged down into the earth." I said, watching as the cabin started to sink into the ground. "Where is Marcus?"

He should have been able to get out before Ethan.

"After you left the door slammed shut." Ethan explained. "He told me to head out first and that he would have to bust his way out."

"He is probably trying to find a weak spot in the cabin." I said as I looked at the sinking cabin.

"Conjure a rope and I will take it to him." Ethan said as he tried to cross the circle.

I doubted that it would be so easy. I watched as the ground inside the magic circle began to split apart and reform into a ring around the cabin with the stones and dirt form a ring pointing to the sky. A portion of the formation began to ripple.

Out of the formation came a gorilla made of stone. It was double the size of a normal man and had glaring red eyes.

I could see that the formation was feeding power to the gorilla.

The gorilla placed its fists on the ground, and I watched as prana moved through the ground towards Ethan. The prana rose and turned the ground into sharp spikes.

"Get out of the circle." I said watching as the spikes tried to pierce Ethan but failed due to his intangibility. "The gorilla is probably there to stop anyone trying to enter."

"Can't you stop this?" Ethan asked, flying outside the circle and looking at me.

The gorilla halted its advance and just watched us as its eyes turned white. It seemed that it would only activate if someone stepped inside the circle.

"Stopping this trap would take time and I believe a lot of mana. If I did that then I would have little to no magic to deal with Bryan afterwards." I said then I started cracking the fingers on my left hand. "Marcus is going to have to get out of this by his own strength."

"The cabin is now halfway buried beneath the earth." Ethan said, pointing.

"A good thing about the cabin being larger on the inside meant that he would have more time to plan an escape." I said with more optimism than I actually felt.

"Do you think that he can burn his way through the cabin?" Ethan asked. "Wouldn't his ring protect him?"

"It would protect him, but you have to remember that he is carrying someone with him." I answered. "If Marcus tried to burn his way through while carrying Stephanie she would definitely be burned to death."

I really did not want Marcus to die in a case that I had brought him in on.

The next second I had to move backwards when a burst of dark wind blew out through the roof. Marcus burst through the hole he had made carrying Stephanie on his back and floating in front of the moon.

I moved to avoid the scattered pieces of the cabin roof falling around us.

"He is such a showoff." I muttered, now annoyed at Marcus as he landed in a crouch with his arms at an angle outside the circle with Stephanie on his back. "You sure took you took your time."

"You say that because you got out early." Marcus said standing and rolling his neck. "Those walls may look flimsy on the outside but inside was a whole other story."

"Marcus be careful." Ethan called out pointing at the gorilla "There is a trap for anyone that crosses the circle."

The cabin had sunken beneath the earth. Yet the circle remained with the gorilla guarding its position.

"We are going to have to do something about this." I said looking at the formation.

"I doubt that this thing is going to be much trouble. Look at it. Daring us with its white eyes to cross the circle." Marcus said as he walked up to the circle pointed with his index and middle fingers at the gorilla. "Lighting bullet."

I heard the sound of crackling and in a few seconds watched as a dark bolt of lightning struck the gorilla's head and shattering it into pieces. The rest of the body followed collapsing into a heap with the magic circle following after.

Marcus stood over the demolished stones pointing to the sky posing in victory.

I let him have the moment. Marcus deserved to have a villain he personally took down tonight. It would shut him up for a while and give me some peace and quiet.

What I did not mention is that it seemed that when the cabin vanished the majority of the power to the gorilla reversed back into the ground sealing up the tunnel that the cabin made.

CHAPTER 23

"Marcus, I want you to try and text Spektral." I said as I looked at the formation and the ground that used to be under the sunken cabin. "He warned us to leave so he should have an idea about what is happening."

"Alright." Marcus said, dropping Stephanie to the ground scattering Geoffrey's ashes as he pulled out his phone and started typing.

"Really?" Ethan asked. "You could be a bit more delicate."

"I would like to remind you that she shot me." Marcus defended as he walked away from Stephanie. "I even pulled her out of a sinking cabin. I think that I have been gentler than most would have in this situation."

"So, the cabin is gone?" Ethan asked as he approached me.

"Burning up in the earth's core is my bet." I said poking a stick at the ground hesitantly as if the ground would split open and drag us down to meet the same fate.

"You would win that bet. According to Spektral Bryan planned on using the trap in case anybody came by after the ritual. We just activated it early." Marcus said as he walked to join us. "I have to admit that these defenses are a wonderful way to get rid of anyone that started poking around in strange places."

"Truly? I wonder what kind of face he would have made when he learned that he was being double- crossed?" I asked as I walked over the ground where the cabin used to be and looked at the moon.

"What do you mean?" Ethan asked.

"It seems that Bryan planned on betraying Geoffrey after all." I said, turning to Ethan while pulling out my plaid pork pie hat and my dragon pipe that blew bubbles. "Let me tell you why."

"Why is he doing a Sherlock Holmes impression?" Ethan asked Marcus.

"You should know the answer to that question by now." Marcus said. "Alex's ego is large enough that you could fit a fleet of blimps inside."

"Silence you philistine." I said, pointing my pipe at him. "Bryan told Geoffrey to head to the basement after he had Stephanie walk to the ritual. If we did not show up and confront him, he would have walked down there without a clue."

Ethan's eyes widened as he understood what I meant. And the ball goes through the net.

"Why did he do this?" Ethan asked.

"He has wild mood swings and lacks ethical values." Marcus guessed.

"It's the classic thieves' double-cross." I said before blowing through the pipe sending bubble into the sky. "Bryan wanted to become immortal. He hunted down a vampire to accomplish that. He decided to get an easier target and somehow made a deal with Geoffrey. He would supply Bryan with a vampire to sacrifice in return for some gift or favor. However, he couldn't trust the secret of his immortality with a stranger. Geoffrey knew his crimes. He could use it as a means to blackmail him. So, he decided to use a method where he could take down his accomplice and keep his secret."

"Geoffrey should have taken our offer." Ethan said, turning to look at the ashes. "He would at least have been alive at the end of this."

"No way." Marcus denied. "Geoffrey got off way too easily."

"Either way it changes nothing for us or our final goal." I said.

"Do you think that Bryan knows what that we ruined his ritual?" Ethan asked.

"No idea." I answered. "He might still be waiting for Stephanie to show up."

"That's a shame. I wanted to hear his rage as he realized he failed after all the innocent people he hurt." Ethan said.

"However, that is to our advantage. We can hunt him while he is stuck waiting for his vampire to arrive to finish the ritual." I said. "Gloating can wait."

I planned to do plenty of it myself.

"There is a problem though." Marcus said. "How are you going to find him if all of his stuff is gone and burning."

It was an important question as it meant I would have to change my plans.

"I still have his I.D." Ethan said pulling out Bryan's wallet. "I was going to toss it at him and explain how we had found him."

"Great. Now we can go and bring down the big bad wizard." Marcus said.

"Marcus I think that you should take Stephanie to the car and drive away from here." I said, tossing him my keys.

"What? Why?" Marcus asked.

"I think that it would be bad after we saved her that she should die again in the battle between me and Bryan." I said, watching as the crimson light began to dim. "Also, if she woke up early, she might get in the way."

"Alright." Marcus said walking to pick up Stephanie. "Where should I be taking her?"

"Take her back to the office." I said. "Tie her up in the backroom."

"You do realize that if I am pulled over and this is taken out of context that this could be considered kidnapping and result in jailtime?" Marcus asked as he lifted Stephanie's body.

"Like you would let any cop arrest you." I said rolling my eyes. "I believe in your ability to figure something out."

The next second they were gone.

"What am I going to be doing?" Ethan questioned.

"You are going to be helping me when I go and try to catch Bryan." I answered before pulling out the scrying crystal and changing the vial for a coin with three holes.

Having someone that could turn invisible would be helpful in case I needed a distraction.

"Wouldn't a button be easier?" Ethan asked.

"This coin represents the three of us. The first hole for the living, the second hole for the dead, and the last hole for the one in between." I said while tying the string and coin together and held it in my right hand and the I.D. in my other. "Invenimus."

The coin began to float and point towards the west.

Now it was time to move.

"How bad do you think that this fight is going to be?" Ethan asked.

"He's killed a lot of people." I answered. "That knife of his probably has a lot of power."

"You must have a better answer." Ethan said. "I thought you wizards might have competitions where you test your magic against each other."

"You are not wrong. It is both a sport and a habit that young people engage in quite often." I acknowledged.

Give people the ability to throw magic around and eventually people are going to want to have a fight with it to learn who is better.

"However normal duels between wizards and witches usually have barriers and spells to protect the participants. Unfortunately, this upcoming fight had none of the usual spells or safeguards in place to protect me."

"Do you have some enchantment that will heal you if something happens?" Ethan asked.

"I have something though I really do not want to use it." I answered as we turned east and came to a bridge that crossed over the river and connected this hill to the one in front and the one to the side.

We took the path to the side. As we came up the hill, we saw the path is marked with lit torches.

"Do you think that if we were watching this in a theater, we would be hearing horror movie music?" Ethan asked.

"Marcus would probably say yes but I prefer to think that we would hear action movie music." I answered as I continued up the path the coin was leading.

"Ahhhhhh!" We heard a voice yell out through the forest.

"Looks like he learned that his ritual has failed. Turn invisible and wait here." I said to him as I continued up the hill.

I crouched behind a tree when I found Bryan pacing around a similar circle to the one outside his cabin. He was standing shirtless and so I could see the tattoos that prevented him from aging covering his body. I looked to the tree and saw the broken pieces of a cell phone.

"Raahhh." Bryan shouted again into the forest.

I noticed that his knife was gripped in his left hand.

"Hello Bryan." I said putting my sunglasses away as I walked from behind the tree. "I have spent a lot of effort trying to find you."

"You must be the detective that Geoffrey warned me about." Bryan said as he turned around. "I take it you are the reason that my vampire has failed to answer my call."

His face looked calm and controlled but I knew it would take little to have his rage overpower him and burst out.

"If you want to know we took down your accomplice and we rescued your victim." I informed him with a smile.

"I hope that you keep that humor when I send you to the grave." Bryan said with a laugh.

"What is this? A nineteen-eighty-six film directed by Russell Mulcahy?" I asked. "There can only be one?"

"There is no other way." Bryan said as his eyes turned into a glare. "You have no idea what you cost me!"

In that moment, I was glad that I wasn't an empath. Just feeling that much hate probably would have made me shiver.

"Calm down. I understand why you started down this dark path but there are other ways to fix you." I said watching for the slightest hint of movement. "We can stop this right here and now but only you have the power to decide that. Turn yourself in and the council can help you."

Despite all that happened I wanted to see if he could be reasoned with.

"You are an arrogant fool." Bryan said glaring. "You act so carefree but your boasting only reveals your fear. After I kill you, I can hunt for another vampire."

"Then you are going to have a problem." I informed him. "I don't plan on dying for a long time."

"You have no idea the power that I have at my command." Bryan said with his right arm curving and conjuring a ball of fire. "I can squash you with the same effort required to end the life of a cockroach."

"You are going to have to catch me first." I said and teleported out of the way.

The fireball hit the tree. The majority of it shattering as it hit the bark but the sparks that hit the base began to climb upwards towards the branches and the leaves.

"You are a walking forest fire. Smokey the bear must hate you." I said looking at the remains.

I couldn't let that fire spread. So, I pointed my wand at it and said "Aqua fons."

Then a spray of water began putting it all out.

Unfortunately, in my desire to put out the fire I stopped paying attention to Bryan. He decided to take a cheap shot and blast me across the field with telekinesis.

As I crashed into the ground, I let out a groan of pain but quickly had to roll to avoid being set on fire.

"You should focus less on the trees and more on me." Bryan said as he tried to slash me with his knife.

I twisted out of the way.

"You know while you are offering advice you should take some as well because I really think you should see someone about that arson problem of yours." I said then started running down the hill.

There was no way that I was going to fight this out in an area that he chose. Right now, the darkness is one of the greatest allies I have.

"Do you really think that you can escape me?" Bryan yelled.

I used strengthening magic to give my legs a boost in running speed. I was running for five minutes before I took a break and hid behind a tree to catch my breath and regain some mana. I took a deep breath as I felt the cool chill of the night. Hearing the hooting of the owls in the trees and the rustle of the leaves. The fact that people did this sort of thing as a sport was something that was truly lost to me.

No gold medal was worth this.

The only reason I was running was so that I would goal is to drain him of most of his magic while keeping mine relatively high.

Magic is generated by the universe and the things that existed within it but that was still only a finite amount of power for each wizard or witch. The more spells you cast the more energy would be lost. People would need time to regain the energy they had lost. Drain too much and eventually you would start tapping into your own life force. The only result from that was noticeable aging or an early death.

"What's the plan?" Ethan asked standing next to me. I hit the bark of the tree to hide my surprise.

"I am heading back to the bridge." I said. "I plan on facing him there."

The water would give me the advantage if he decided to keep using fire.

"Come out you coward!" Bryan shouted into the night as he searched. "Have you no pride as a wizard?"

That was funny coming from someone with less than a year of training. I doubted that he even understood the culture that he was now a part of.

"What should I do?" Ethan asked.

"Go and place this on the ground a few feet from the bridge." I said, handing him a circular ring. "This is a trap that will keep him contained."

The ring contained an enchantment that would bind his magic once he stepped inside the area. It is what the magic council used during trials while they questioned questionable wizards/ witches.

"Alright." Ethan said as he turned invisible.

"All that power and you can't catch one man." I yelled at him before I started running again to the west.

"You want to test me?" Bryan yelled. "Then let's see how you deal with this."

I glanced back to see what he planned to do. When I heard straining sounds from the ground, I realized that he intended to pull the tress from the ground and send them at me.

Clearly, I could not let that happen.

"Vehementi Impetu." I said as I came from behind a tree and knocked him forward to the ground and then while he was getting back up, I started running to the bridge.

"Did you place it?" I asked Ethan the moment that I arrived.

"Yes." Ethan said.

"Is this where you want your final resting place to be?" Bryan asked floating above me.

Arrows of fire formed around him.

"If you mean that I want this place to be our battlefield? Then yes." I said pointing my wand at him. "I mean our fight wouldn't be interesting if I beat you while hiding behind a rock."

"You sound like you truly believe that you are capable of doing that." Bryan said spreading his fingers in front of him and launching the fire arrows. "I will kill you in the most painful way that is possible."

"Aqua nesfe." I said waving my wand in an arc from left to right causing a shield of water to rise from the river.

The moment that the fire arrows met the water barrier a field of steam exploded around us.

"Manus Terrae." I said, raising my wand up with both hands.

Giant hands rose from the earth and tried to grasp Bryan.

"Is this all you got?" Bryan shouted as he began to levitate off of the ground into the sky to escape from the spell. "Where is all your boasting now? Take this as a lesson that you should have never interfered in my plans."

As he rose above the trees, he pointed his knife upwards and conjured a giant orb of fire. Through the orb a giant snake began to materialize.

If that wasn't created in an effort to try and kill me, I would appreciate how cool that looked.

"Like the Italian Stallion once said "It ain't about how hard you hit. It's about how hard you can get hit and keep moving forward; how much you can take and keep moving forward." After everything I have gone through my desire for justice and revenge have long passed my common sense." I said while I moved my wand in a circle with both hands. "Ventus turbinis vasti."

A huge tornado formed on the other side of the bridge and began to move closer towards him. If he was going to use fire, then I was going to use wind.

Either combustion would make him explode or the tornado would suck away all of his oxygen.

The moment that the tornado came into contact with the fire snake they combined forming a supernatural disaster. Looking at the devastation that was being caused as the flaming whirlwind moved, I winced. There were scorch marks where the fire was spreading, and scars created by the movement of the tornado.

I really had to fix this when we were done.

The tornado was doused when water from the river was pulled up poured down to it. There was an explosion of steam as the opposing elements matched.

"Not even that tornado you created can stop me." Bryan said as he panted in the sky.

I ignored his bragging and fought the urge to smile. It seems that the plan is working.

"You can deny it however you want. I can see you struggling." I said, pointing my wand to the river at my side. "Aqua Impetus Gladiorum."

I conjured twenty swords of ice and sent them flying at him. Impetus Gladiorum is a spell I didn't get to use on people often as unless you were immortal because being stabbed by a swarm of swords usually resulted in the death of regular people.

Bryan, even if he wasn't immortal, was a person that I believe I could use this on and I wouldn't feel bad at all.

He didn't even look troubled, he just stopped flying and let himself fall to the ground but stopped before he actually crashed.

"Geoffrey told me how fond you are of swords." Bryan said adjusting his position. "Besides their design I am not impressed."

He gave me a grin as he thought he had escaped my spell and showed me how much smarter he was than me.

"Don't worry you will be thinking differently when this battle is over!" I shouted and pointed up for him to look at all my swords that were pointed down at him held by telekinesis.

"You have hurt so many people with your knife. Let's see how you like being stavved." I taunted.

"You won't ever get the chance." Bryan said, pointing his knife at me.

The tip of the knife began to glow with a dark red that grew with each second.

"This light is pure mana." Bryan said. "With the amount that I have it is possible for me to fire them off like cannonballs."

"Then the question is just who will be faster." I said, pointing up at the twenty swords floating above him. "I'm willing to test my luck."

"Don't you dare." Bryan said as he looked back at me.

As the swords fell down at him, he used his mana to create a shield to protect himself from the swords falling down and piercing him like a rather violent version of darts.

"I have never met someone as annoying as you!" Bryan shouted at me. "Before I kill you, I am going to rip your eyes out, feed them to you, and sew your mouth shut!"

He clearly realized that he was losing control and started lashing out due to it. I wondered how long it would take before he just started screaming nonsense.

When I read passages in his journal, I learned that the man had major control issues and when you take the control away from someone like that they could only go so far before they began to have a mental breakdown and go on a rampage.

"Really because you were going to let me off so easy before?" I asked as I ran at him while using telekinesis to summon an ice sword to my right hand.

I had to duck a telekinetically flung sword. I looked behind me and saw that the sword was embedded very deep in a tree. I frowned at him.

"That was close" I complained at him rubbing my neck. "You could have taken my head off."

"That was the idea!" Bryan shouted at me as he defended with one of my own swords.

"You should be glad that we are dueling over a river of water and not one made of lava." I said as I used a downward strike. "It did not end so well for the last guy."

"Do you ever shut up?" Bryan asked as we clashed swords and moved farther down the bridge. "I refuse to be stopped by some man-child with the personality of a five-year-old that wishes to play detective!"

There had to be a limit to how rude a person could be.

"I am not pretending. I took my tests and received my license." I defended.

He took a few wild swings that chipped my blade but did not deter me.

"You should be mindful of your rage. Anger and hate can only lead to suffering." I said jumping atop the bridge railing to avoid a downward swing.

He was on the defensive now blocking and moving back with each strike.

"How have you managed to live this long?" Bryan asked. "I barely know you and yet I want to hear you scream as you are ripped apart by horses."

The angrier he got the wilder his swings became. It was always sad when smart accomplished people went crazy.

Usually because that same insanity led them to becoming homicidal.

With a quick burst of strengthening magic, I charged at him and stabbed him through the foot making sure that it reached into the bridge trapping him.

"Aahhh." Bryan yelled in pain.

"Fulgur manus." I said sending streams of lightning from my empty hand while jumping back to gain some distance and watched as he began to twitch as he was shocked with the voltage equivalent of a taser.

I wasn't fond of using lightning from a wand, it just looked weird in my opinion. Proper magical lighting moved in arcs that came from the fingers.

After three minutes I stopped and moved over to him.

"Are you ready to surrender?" I asked.

He mumbled something I could not hear. Probably because he was still getting over the shock.

I figured I should help him. So, I walked over to him, pulled the sword out, and kicked him over onto his back.

"Are you ready to surrender?" I repeated.

"Never." Bryan growled.

He raised his hand lifting me off of the ground and then sending me to the other railing.

I groaned as my back made contact.

"That is going to hurt in the morning." I said as I tried to regain my balance.

"You found amusement in stabbing me?" Bryan asked me with fake curiosity as he traced his knife along my face. "Let's see how you feel when the blade is in my hand."

The desire for murder and revenge cleat in his crazy eyes.

"The difference is that you deserved it." I said looking at the knife.

"Keep talking it just makes me want to kill you even more." Bryan said with a glare as he stabbed me in the side.

When Ethan had described the sensation during his murder, I had guessed the pain but actually feeling it was a whole other thing.

It started as a throbbing sensation that started from my side and felt like it was spreading through my body. The worst part came next. A burning sensation spread from the knife, and I could feel my body starting to heat up.

"I usually put my sacrifices in a trance during the ritual, so they feel as little pain as possible when they die but this time, I want you to experience every moment." Bryan growled as he moved back.

I ignored the pain and focused on the fact that he was now separated from his knife. Then I started smiling.

No matter how much it hurts to do so.

"You have something to say?" Bryan questioned as he tilted his head. "What, what is so funny?"

"Vehementi Impetu." I said as I cupped my hand and blasted him off of the bridge and close to the trap.

Now that I was free, I moved to pull the knife out. When I clasped my hand around the handle of the blade, I felt a deep chill at the dark mana coating the weapon.

I felt like if I looked at it, I could imagine the blood coating my hand.

How mad must Bryan be to hold this weapon proudly and not shiver in disgust?

"Are you alright?" Ethan asked as he appeared and walked to me.

"I will be fine in a minute." I said before shaking my head to clear my mind.

My next move was to pull a small vial containing Marcus's blood. "I told you I was prepared."

Vampire blood held healing properties. From horrifying injuries like horrible burns, car accidents, animal attacks or worse, vampire blood could bring you back to a healthy condition. The only downside was the risk of being killed and transitioning.

I had Marcus prepare a few vials before we left in case something unexpected happened. I stabbed my thigh and exhaled as the pain vanished.

"No more playing around." I said as I flipped the knife and placed the handle in front of him. "You want to come and help me push him to the trap?"

"Really?" Ethan asked.

"He no longer has his focus." I said. "He should be a lot weaker now."

"Yes." Ethan answered after grasping the knife. "Not to mention wouldn't it feel great stabbing him with the weapon that he used to end my life."

"Sound like a good time? Then follow me." I said jumping over the bridge and to the land where I had tossed Bryan.

The strengthening magic prevented injury and kept my landing stable. A small crater formed around my landing point.

"I won't let you rob me of my future!" Bryan yelled as he ran at me.

I blocked his fist and returned a punch that hit him upside the head.

Then while he was reeling from that I turned so that I had his held behind his back.

"Give up this is over." I said. "It's time for you to pay for those that you have hurt."

"Don't start some speech about fairness. Or lives cut tragically short." Bryan said, trying to break free. "Was it fair that I developed a fatal disease? Was it fair that the hospital charged ridiculous amounts of money for treatments that cannot fix me?"

"Your point?" I asked.

"Life isn't fair." Bryan said. "You can only deal with the cards that you are dealt. At least there is a reason that my victims died."

"Fine. I won't give you a speech." I said with a sigh. "Ethan where did you place the trap?"

"Right here." Ethan said pointing at a location two feet away.

"Great." I said as I shoved him to the area and watched as the prison band activated. "Bryan, you have walked down a dark road. Maybe one day you will see that there were other options."

The ring activated the moment that Bryan entered the circle. The white circles glowed outside the circle as they surrounded him. The triangles inside the circle sent white strands covered in runes around him covering him like a mummy. The circles began to converge on him, and the wrappings faded revealing Bryan's body.

The ring would prevent him activating magic for an hour. That gave me plenty of time to put him in his temporary containment room while I contacted the council.

"However right now here is someone that wants some justice." Ethan said as he approached.

"What are you doing?" I asked, looking at the knife in his hand.

"He stole my life to extend his." Ethan said before moving to look Bryan in his eyes. "So, before you are arrested, I want you to experience the true cost of that life."

Ethan moved to stab the knife through Bryan's chest.

"Wait." I said using telekinesis to freeze him in place.

"What are you doing?" Ethan asked. "Let me go."

"Not if you are going to stab him." I said.

"Are you going to tell me that he does not deserve this?" Ethan asked. "After everything that he put you through. After everything that he took from me and his other victims.

I understood Ethan's desire. A lot of what I had done during this case had been driven by a mixture of pride and revenge. Not to mention where I planned to put him. A part of me would like to let this happen but I couldn't.

Not to mention that it would probably screw with Ethan's afterlife judgement. I was not sure, but I liked to believe that revenge-killing and murder would have an effect on it.

"If you stab him, it is likely that he will die, and I won't get paid." I said. "How about a compromise?"

"Like what?" Ethan asked.

"I can cast a spell on the knife." I said. "That way he feels the pain of everyone that he ever stabbed."

"How bad will it hurt?" Ethan asked frowning but no longer advancing.

"Every second." I said. "It would be like all of Bryan's victims were taking revenge on him by making him feel their pain at the moment that he took their lives."

"You can't do this." Bryan said with his eyes wide.

"Very well." Ethan said, ignoring him.

"Hand me the knife and I can begin." I said, releasing him and holding my hand out.

"Here." Ethan said handing me back the knife.

I placed the knife on the ground and turned it parallel to Bryan.

"I would advise you to grit your teeth, but I doubt that you will be able to even do that." I said as I pointed my wand at the knife. "Tiac ariaj."

In the first few seconds Bryan started screaming as he fell to his knees.

After four minutes he stopped moving.

"Is he dead?" Ethan asked as he approached the body.

"No look." I said using telekinesis to lift his head.

A quick glance at his eyes and you could see the pain he was in. You could just imagine a miniature version of himself screaming as hard as he could in his mind.

"We did it." Ethan said as he sunk to his knees on the ground. "It is finally over."

"Yes, the case of the cursed blade is officially closed." I said pulling out the snow globe that I had stored in my workshop and pointed my wand at Bryan. "Magni Adamai."

We watched as he got sucked into the snow globe.

"What are you planning on doing to him now?" Ethan asked as he walked over to look at the snow globe.

"I told you that I had a plan for the abandoned warehouse." I said with a smirk. "Imago Visum."

That spell created a screen and let him get a closer look of the inside. Of the warehouse which showed Bryan inside the ritual circle that we had found earlier.

"You put him inside of his own ritual?" Ethan asked as he looked at the screen.

"Yup now he is trapped inside of a cage inside of a cage. I call it cageception." I told them. "Here catch."

I tossed the snow globe to Ethan.

"What are you doing now?" Ethan asked.

"Now I have to hide all the damage that Bryan and I have caused before we leave." I said as I walked to the east bridge. "Figere damnum."

I chanted with my wand moving like mickey mouse in that old cartoon where he was a wizard with magic gloves.

It was a shame that I would not be able to learn what type of books Bryan was reading from. It would help a lot when he was brought to trial.

CHAPTER 24

"You are going to dig a hole in my floor if you keep pacing like that." I said as I wrapped the strands of hair around the doll.

The spell I am preparing is based on demon puppetry. The skill of a yokai from ancient Japan. The hair would allow the doll to take on the appearance of the owner. This spell involved a wooden carved doll and the hair of the person you wish to impersonate. The body-double's life span lasted as long as magic is poured into it.

Given that I had Bryan trapped I had more than enough to cast the spell.

With the story Nurse Ramirez gave about Bryan the cops would assume that his sickness led to despair. When the detectives investigated his house they would discover very disturbing poetry about life, death, and memory.

It would lead the cops to believe that he went on a murder spree to be remembered and an insane idea that by doing these ritualistic murders he would live longer because of the lives that he had stolen. When it was rendered inert from lack of magic it would go on the record that he died from his disease.

Marcus would make sure that the coroner did not look any deeper into the matter.

"When did you say that they were going to arrive?" Ethan asked.

"No need to worry the council wizards are on their way." I told him before putting down the carving and glancing at the snow globe on my desk. "They take calls concerning dark wizards very seriously."

"How can you not be worried?" Ethan asked. "Each second that passes is another chance that Bryan could use to break free."

"Relax. He is in a secure location, and I doubt there is anybody interested in freeing him." I said giving the snow globe a brief shake with my free hand.

"What about Spektral?" Ethan argued. "Bryan may have lost but that might be what Spektral believes he needed. A way to give him a new ambition. A hook into a new season He could be on his way to free him right now."

"If Spektral wants to interfere in a council arrest then I can just kick back and watch as the council hunts him down." I said.

It took passing a series of complicated tests to be granted their jobs and each year they had to have an evaluation so they could keep getting paid that massive amount. I saw just one of those evaluation tests once and it told me I was nowhere close to their league and given the effort required I did not want to be.

Hearing the doorknob turn I glanced to the side.

"It seems that the waiting will be what turns Ethan into a vengeful poltergeist." Marcus said as he walked inside then hesitated before turning to me. "Are you listening to the Beach Boys?"

"I find the song Kokomo soothing at times like this." I answered. "Did you get enough sandwiches?"

"I got fifteen." Marcus said while turning the bag upside down and dumping the sandwiches on the table.

"That should take an hour to finish." I said with a smile rising from my desk.

"Seriously?" Ethan asked.

"You should come and get one." I said stretching out my hand. "Seven are bacon and eight are spicy chicken."

"The fun in the game is guessing which is which." Marcus said. "I am ahead with two wins."

"This will be my day." I said moving to wrap my fingers around a sandwich.

"I am not hungry at the moment." Ethan said with a judgmental scowl.

He was going to ruin my appetite if I let him.

"If you need to keep yourself busy read a book." I said using telekinesis to move a book off the shelf to him.

"Nezobi and The Hunt for The Golden Pyramid?" Ethan asked after it fell into his hands "I have never heard of this book."

"No surprise. It is from the other side of the Alter-Plane." I said unwrapping the sandwich. "It's an adventure story that should keep you occupied."

"Which do you think that is?" Marcus asked.

"I believe that it is spicy chicken." I said moving to take a bite.

I felt a surge of prana. I am going to really annoyed if Ethan was right and Spketral decided to show up.

"Alex, look out behind you." Ethan called out.

I teleported back to my desk to drop my sandwich and grab my wand as I looked up to see what caused the warning. It seemed that while I was going to grab a sandwich a giant orb appeared in the room in front of the door.

On the orb is the symbol of the magic council. Four petals around a circle and on the inside of the circle is a pentacle.

"The inspectors have finally arrived." I said while placing my wand back on the desk. The next moment I looked to see a man and woman pair walking through the orb.

The man is tall with black hair that was white at the base and the woman has brown hair that was turning black. They are wearing blue jackets over their black bodysuits. They wore violet gloves with the symbol of the council on them.

"I am Inspector Dekker Jordan, and this is my partner, Inspector Heather Anderson." Inspector Jordan said.

His eyes are an electric blue that looked like they could see through you and freeze you solid in the attempt. He also has a series of stiches going down the right side of his face.

"The council was notified that you have captured a dark wizard." Inspector Anderson said.

She had glittering eyes the color of cold jade.

"He is in here." I said as I raised the snow globe off of my desk. "His name is Bryan Mercer, and he has murdered nineteen people with sacrificial magic in order to gain power and immortality."

"I am one of them." Ethan said as he raised a finger.

"The suspect will be questioned to make sure that you are telling the truth." Inspector Anderson said with her head having followed my travel. "If you are payment will be sent to you. If not, then you will suffer the consequences of wasting the council's time. You are aware of the punishment for a false report?"

The punishment for reporting a false call to the council is five years in jail.

"Yes." I said using telekinesis to send the snow globe floating in front of them.

"Very well. Do not leave town. We may have some questions for you and your group regarding your involvement in these events." Inspector Jordan said.

They walked back into the orb that began and contrary to my assumption it exploded into a bright light. It was worse than staring at the sun for ten seconds because a kid at the playground dared you to see how long you could last.

"Seriously?" Marcus asked. "Are they trying to blind us permanently?"

I was too busy rubbing my eyes to see him speak. "The thing about council wizards/witches is that they are as eccentric as they are powerful."

"You don't say?" Ethan asked. "I know that we shouldn't form opinion on people based on assumptions but there is just something about them that I found unsettling."

"Given how they left I would say that your feelings have some merit." Marcus said as he stopped blinking.

"Stop complaining guys." I said feeling cheerful. "Now that we have handed off Bryan to the council, we call the police to have them arrest the demon puppet."

"Before we do this, I want to convince you one more time to go over our other options." Marcus said as he ran to the whiteboard carrying our plans for the demon puppet.

"What's wrong with the plan we have now?" I asked.

The current plan seemed simple enough.

"The problem is that it is boring." Marcus said as he grabbed the marker and began writing. "My first idea is that we have Bryan storm into a bank. Maybe he takes a couple hostages. The negotiator arrives and Bryan demands a helicopter in return for the release of the hostages. The negotiator agrees to the terms. However, it is a trap, When Bryan entered the helicopter, he would find that the pilot was Detective Langdon and, to his surprise, he would be arrested."

"That sounds like a waste of my time and mana." I objected.

"Hurtful." Marcus said as he dropped his head.

"It also seems way too complicated. Even if we could control all variables there is a chance of something going wrong." I said. "One of the hostages could get hurt. Someone could have a heart attack; someone could try to be a hero."

"Fine if you are worried about controlling everything here is my second idea." Marcus said as he crossed out his first idea and began writing below it. "We have this end at Bryan's house. He would refuse to surrender and charge at them only for Detective O'Connell to shoot him ending his reign of terror."

"All your ideas sound like something that would work better in a movie." Ethan said. "Why don't we just have Bryan's double confess it all in writing? No judge or court of law would possibly ignore that."

That excited Marcus as he started writing again.

"Just imagine if we set up this whole court day. Bright and sunny with no clouds in the sky. The hour before the trial starts, we get him to stand in front of cameras and when he proclaims his innocence, we cause a giant bolt of lightning to strike him. Or imagine that he is standing on trial and when he claims he is not guilty it looks like his heart just gave out." Marcus said. "It would probably be in all of the newspapers and on all the news stations. They would be talking about it for months."

"I vote no to both of your choices. They might give him an insanity defense. Too many people would watch him then." I denied shaking my head.

"Aren't you going to flip the coin to choose which option that you would prefer?" Marcus asked.

"No." I said. "For this decision I am certain on the path that I wish to tread."

It was best that the death of Bryan's double got as little attention as possible. I wanted him to vanish as quickly as a pigeon in a snowstorm.

"Alright." Marcus said sadly as he walked to the phone on his desk with the speed of a snail. "We will go with your idea."

He started pressing buttons and put the phone on speaker.

"What do you want?" Detective O'Connell demanded.

"We wanted to talk our lucky leprechaun." Marcus said clearly cheering up now that he got to bother someone. "See how your investigation is going."

"I am rather busy at the moment trying to find a lead on this Bryan Mercer, you and your client led us to." Detective O'Connell answered with annoyance in his voice.

"Well, I have some great news for you. We have already found Bryan." Marcus said. "It was a citizen's arrest."

"Really?" Detective O'Connell asked.

"He admitted to everything." I said, walking to Marcus's desk. "How he hunted his victims, the locations that he placed them, and even the method of how he killed them."

"How did you get him to do that?" Detective O'Connell asked.

"We confronted him with our suspicions, and he admitted to everything." I said. "He crumbled like a cookie dunked in milk. I think it might be because I found a four-leaf clover on the way to his house."

"We have him sitting in a chair in the office." Marcus said. "He was willing to be taken to the police station, but Alex believes that will cause problems. I believe it is just because he is afraid of the spotlight. He can be so shy."

"I just do not want to cause issues with police detectives that I want to get along with." I argued. "We will be on our way." Detective O'Connell grudgingly.

"See the two of you then." Marcus said as he hung up the phone. "Happy?"

"Very much so." I said before teleporting in front of an empty chair and placed the wooden carving down.

I watched as the wooden carving began to grow and transform into an exact copy of Bryan.

"Ethan." I said, turning to the spirit. "You should try to find something fun to do with your remaining hours."

"What?" Ethan asked.

"We agreed to work together to solve your murder. Now that we have eventually you are going to have to return to the Final Station. The place you were before I summoned you." I said walking to him. "I figure that you might have some things you want to do beforehand."

"What about the police?" Ethan asked.

"Marcus and I can handle that." I said, handing him some money.

It was not like he could meet them anyway.

"He just wants you gone so he can focus on his goal of getting Detective Langdon's number." Marcus said.

"Shut it." I said using telekinesis to force one of the sandwiches off of the table and into his mouth.

"You can try to silence me, but you can't silence the truth." Marcus said as he pulled the sandwich away.

"Either way it is not a bad idea." Ethan said wrapping his fingers around the money. "There are many things I have to do if I wish to rest in peace."

We watched as he walked out the door.

"That kid is so dramatic." Marcus said.

"Exactly." I confirmed then looked at the backroom door. "Anyway, how do you think we should deal with Stephanie?"

"What do you mean?" Marcus asked.

"I mean when she wakes up do you think that we are going to have another new enemy?" I asked. "We know that Geoffrey lied and manipulated her, but she does not believe that. The last thing that she knows is that we had taken away her boyfriend and broken her neck. Not to mention that you killed her in the first place. Those things hardly seem to be something one could get over so easily. Even more so when she has her emotions and fears amplified due to her vampirism. The moment that she wakes up she might start plotting a way to get her revenge on us."

"Funny that you think of that now and not when she was unconscious in the cabin." Marcus said, looking at the door.

"I did not want to make life or death decisions while hunting an evil wizard." I said shrugging. "The guilt might have distracted me at a horrible moment."

"Either way it is good that we think about this now." Marcus said. "If you are concerned about her future plans, you could show her your memoires of the events that happened after she died."

"You mean hearing Geoffrey boasting about how he planned to kill her and make her the vampire sacrifice for the ritual." I said.

"Yes." Marcus answered. "It might break her, but it will allow us the opportunity to build her back up into an ally."

"It could be useful if it works." I said. "After the police pick up Bryan, we can work on her. Hopefully it all works out and you can show her how to survive this sudden turn her life has taken."

"It should be fun." Marcus said clapping his hands then rubbing them together with a smile. "When I was alive, I was working to be a teacher."

A part of me feared what I might be unleashing upon this world.

May this be the universe constantly felt like punishing me?

Not something I had done but something that I would inspire. An Idea so horrible that it had to punish me beforehand to even get close to appropriate payback.

CHAPTER 25

"I guess it is time for me to go?" Ethan asked with a sigh as he looked at the magic circle.

It would not be wrong to admit that there is an awkward feeling in the air. I had gotten started on this case because his aunt had gotten worried and hired me to bring him home to her safely, but he was dead, and the client is now missing.

It had been incredibly awkward getting him to talk about what type of burial he wanted for his body.

"Yes." I answered as I looked at Ethan standing in the summoning circle. "I hope you managed to do what you needed."

When I told him to enjoy the day the sun had been rising. Hours had gone by and now the moon swayed over the sky without equal.

"I took some time to truly experience some of the sights of Philadelphia." Ethan said. "I walked around center city, fed some ducks at the zoo, and looked in on some of my friends."

"Did you talk to them?" I asked.

If he had, then I needed to know what kind of damage control is required. The risk to the city is too great to leave events to chance.

"That was too difficult. I was hoping that you would give me time to write a letter and then you can send it to them." Ethan said.

"No problem." I said using apportation to summon a pen and some paper. "Write down their addresses and I will use a spell to make sure that they receive your words in their dreams."

"Alright." Ethan said sitting crossed-legged and starting to write.

I heard sniffles and watched as tears started forming.

He paused his writing to clear his eyes, but I could see his hand starting to shake.

This was even worse than before and the awkwardness only increased as the seconds passed. A surge of sadness grew in me as I watched this spirit try to put his final words together. I decided to close my eyes and turned my thoughts back to work.

Even with Bryan arrested and in custody there are many questions left unanswered.

Like why did Spektral reveal magic to Bryan? Why instruct him on how to curse that knife? Why send him down the path of dark magic with a ritual that resulted in him killing so many people?

Normally I prefer my mysteries to be more like Saturday morning cartoons. The clues are obvious, the bad guy's motive is clear, and the ending fits into a nice little box.

Right now, I had none of those and these are questions that needed to be answered.

"You do not have to worry when you return to the afterlife station. I will try to find out what happened to your aunt." I said before opening my eyes.

"You really think that she is still alive? That neither Bryan nor Spektral got rid of my aunt in an attempt to cover their tracks?" Ethan asked, then he turned to looked up to the ceiling. "Maybe I will run into her when you send me back?

"Dark optimism is not the solution." I said shaking my head. "More importantly that is quitter talk."

"What is so wrong about that?" Ethan asked. "I believe that mood would fit the situation."

"You are trying to avoid despair but that answer only has power as long as you can force yourself to believe the lie." I said. "Self-hypnosis is a powerful thing, but I doubt it can last an eternity. More importantly embracing a delusion to ignore reality is not healthy."

"What else can I do?" Ethan asked.

"In situations where you feel like things are falling apart you can rely on others." I said fighting the shiver that went down my spine as I felt like an afterschool special. "You can believe that I will try my hardest to find out what happened to your aunt. Afterwards I will summon you back to inform you what happened."

"Are you certain that you want to put your life at risk for this?" Ethan asked. "Aren't you just hoping that the next missing person case you have is just a missing person? Or maybe a simple robbery?"

Those would be cases that I would look forward to, but I had a feeling that this Spektral would be a problem for my health and wellbeing.

So, I would hunt him down first.

"You have watched as I ran into danger this past week to get justice for the dead." I said. "How I charged headfirst into a vampire's fangs to stop Bryan's scheme. I will make sure that I discover what happened to your aunt. Whether the result is good or bad you can face the truth."

"Very well." Ethan said as he stood up and held out the papers in his hand.

The moment after I apported the papers to a nearby desk I destroyed the magic circle on the floor that had been keeping him bound to this plane of existence.

"It was cool working with you." Ethan said as he started fading away. "After all, how many spirits can say that they worked with a wizard and a vampire to catch his killer?"

"I hope whatever afterlife awaits you is a peaceful one." I said.

"I hope that whatever next case you have is easier than this one." Ethan said.

"Me too. It would be fun hunting an art thief." I said trying to give a smile until he finished fading away.

Left alone in the vast whiteness of my workshop I had to hurry and get out or I would start being broody and depressed. I put the necklace back onto a shelf and walked to my library.

After everything what I needed to relax is a good book.

9 781959 483649